Beatriz Serrano

DISCONTENT

Beatriz Serrano is a writer and a journalist who has written for publications such as BuzzFeed, *Vanity Fair, GQ, Harper's Bazaar, S Moda,* and *Vogue.* She works for *El País* and, along with writer Guillermo Alonso, co-directs the podcast *Arsénico Caviar,* which won the Ondas Prize for best conversational podcast. *Discontent* is her first novel. She currently lives in Madrid.

DISCONTENT

A Novel

Beatriz Serrano

Translated by Mara Faye Lethem

VINTAGE BOOKS

A DIVISION OF PENGUIN RANDOM HOUSE LLC

NEW YORK

Published by Vintage Books, a division of
Penguin Random House LLC, 1745 Broadway, New York, New York.
Originally published in Spain by Editorial Planeta S.A.U., Barcelona,
in 2023. Copyright © 2023 by Beatriz Serrano.

Vintage and colophon are registered
trademarks of Penguin Random House LLC.

Library of Congress Cataloging-in-Publication Data
Names: Serrano, Beatriz, 1989– author. | Lethem, Mara, translator.
Title: Discontent : a novel / Beatriz Serrano; translated by Mara Faye Lethem.
Other titles: Descontento. English
Description: First edition. | New York: Vintage Books,
a division of Penguin Random House LLC, 2025.
Identifiers: LCCN 2024049891 | ISBN 9798217006762 (trade paperback) |
ISBN 9798217006779 (ebook)
Subjects: LCSH: Women—Spain—Fiction. | Anxiety in women—Fiction. |
Work environment—Fiction. | LCGFT: Novels.
Classification: LCC PQ6719.E845395 D4713 2025 |
DDC 863/.7—dc23/eng/20241108
LC record available at https://lccn.loc.gov/2024049891

Vintage Books Trade Paperback ISBN: 979-8-217-00676-2
eBook ISBN: 979-8-217-00677-9

Book design by Nicholas Alguire

penguinrandomhouse.com | vintagebooks.com

Printed in the United States of America
3rd Printing

The authorized representative in the EU for product safety and
compliance is Penguin Random House Ireland, Morrison
Chambers, 32 Nassau Street, Dublin D02 YH68, Ireland,
https://eu-contact.penguin.ie.

For my parents, Javier Serrano and Lola Molina.
And for everyone who wakes up, every day,
with no desire to go to work.

I was looking for a job and then I found a job
And heaven knows I'm miserable now
　　　—The Smiths, "Heaven Knows I'm Miserable Now"

If you put some effort into appearing normal, you can save
yourself a lot of time, during which you can be what you
want to be in peace.
　　　　　—Georgi Gospodinov, *The Physics of Sorrow,*
　　　　　　　　　　　tr. Angela Rodel

Part One

LOOKING INSIDE IS DANGEROUS

I

For a brief moment back in 2016, the internet's obsession was the physical and mental well-being of an English YouTuber named Marina Joyce. Joyce, who was girlish and princesslike, with long blond ringlets and huge blue eyes, uploaded innocent videos where she tried on pastel-colored clothes, opened gifts sent to her by different brands, or ate sweets she thought were exotic because they came from Asia. And because the internet's blurring of boundaries often means you can't discern whether you are viewing erotic content or family content (or, perhaps, both at the same time), a widely disparate community followed her—from little girls who wanted to wear the same pink dresses to bald men in their fifties who probably masturbated to videos of her eating ice cream.

But after a while, her followers began detecting subtle changes in her behavior. In one of her videos, Marina Joyce was at a party, smiling at the camera and showing off her outfit, but something in the way she walked around (languid and listless) or the way she responded to questions (taking about three seconds too long to grasp them) set off all the alarms. This gave rise to a conspiracy theory, according to which Joyce had been kidnapped by her boyfriend or by a cult (it was unclear which) and was being abused and forced to upload videos against her will.

The evidence shown by these internet detectives consisted of short video clips where, if you paid attention, you could hear a subtle and whispered "help me" that, apparently, she would have added in the editing. There were also videos of Joyce seemingly looking at the back of the room, somewhere behind her camera, in order to get the approval of her captor while she answered questions from her followers. Fans also showed screenshots where her limbs appeared to have bruises, scratches, or small wounds. This was irrefutable evidence. Marina Joyce continued to act friendly and cheerful, but behind the smiles, she often looked sleepy, dazed, or drugged. Some screenshots, which ended up on forums or posted to Twitter accounts dedicated exclusively to the exciting case, showed subliminal messages she was supposedly using to draw people's attention. These messages were hidden among the beautiful white lacquered shelves covered in brand gifts that were always in the background of her videos. Her followers, and those who had followed the trending hashtag #SaveMarinaJoyce, ended up calling the Metropolitan Police to rescue her. The Met went to her house but found nothing suspicious and left.

I'm thinking about Marina Joyce in the cold meeting room I've reserved for a call with the accounts team to talk about the Christmas campaign. I'm also thinking that, if the police were alerted by a loved one and arrived here right now, they wouldn't find anything suspicious either—just a woman in an office, like Marina was just a woman in a room. Only my true fans would notice unsettling changes in my behavior meeting after meeting, day after day, video after video. They would discuss it online in forums and post long explanatory threads on Twitter. Perhaps I'd even be a trending topic for a few hours. The same woman who used to have fun behind her camera now seems sleepy, dazed, and even drugged.

And none of their assumptions would be wrong. It's the end of August, and I only come into the office to lower my air-conditioning bill. It's Monday again and I haven't made progress on any Christmas projects, but I know I've logged enough videocall time to convince the accounts team I've got several things underway. I set my laptop, a cup of water, and a notebook on a large table that I've strategically positioned so natural light illuminates my face. If I've learned anything from YouTubers, it's how to direct the camera in a meeting. I like to reserve this room because it has a neutral background. After this meeting, I could record my reaction to videos of cats gagging when they smell broccoli or a tutorial on the perfect makeup for both a job interview and a first date. Before logging in, I try to imagine how I would greet my followers, but I can't think of anything that doesn't make me sound like an idiot.

The accounts team logs in right on time, and the stupid dance of platitudes that precedes every meeting at every company around the world begins. "How are you girls?" "Are you in Madrid or . . . ?" "Working from the beach isn't really working." "Super busy, can't complain." "Life is good." "Tons of work, which is great." "You can already see my tan." "I'm available for you guys 24/7." "Are your kids there? Tell them I say hi, they're so cute!" I smile, I participate, I make up stuff. I talk about summer plans I don't have with people who don't exist. A few days in Marbella at my friend Pitu's house. A quick trip to San Sebastián with my man. Although I don't know if it's too early to call him "my man," I declare mysteriously. Yes, I tell them, he's Basque, I've always liked guys who could be lumber-jacks. And they all laugh. Simple jokes, clichés served up as a refreshing alcohol-free aperitif to prolong meetings without really getting to work.

Someone takes the lead—"OK, girls, let's get started"—
and the meeting officially begins. They talk about deadlines,
brainstorming, giving this or that a try, WOW factor, making a story go viral, and some even mention the word "disrup-
tion." They talk about what the client is expecting from us this
year—always "a lot" but never anything specific—and how this
Christmas campaign is more important than ever. In each of
the four years I've been at this office, I've been told that *this*
Christmas campaign is more important than ever. I nod with
my brow furrowed and say, "Can you repeat that, Monica?"
while I doodle a penis with little arms in my Moleskine. "Do
we have any more briefings on the lipstick?" I ask, then let
them fight among themselves for ten more minutes over who
will call the client to request information I don't really need.

We've been clowning around for forty minutes. Work is just
a role you play and I've mastered it perfectly. I know the jokes
that always break the ice. I know what to ask to seem attentive
and interested. And I know what to say to make the time flow
faster, without actually doing anything, until I can go home
at six.

While they talk to each other, I open Twitter and watch a
video of a pet raccoon eating a birthday cake. The cake has
three candles, but the raccoon seems afraid of the flame, so a
human helps blow them out for him; then the raccoon starts
eating the cake with his tiny hands. I retweet it. I google if it's
possible to have a raccoon in an apartment in Madrid. Then
I google how long raccoons live. When I read that a wild raccoon can live between two and three years, I feel unexpectedly
disappointed.

"When do you think you could show us something, Marisa?"
asks one of them.

I close the raccoon tab and look at the meeting again. Spe-
cifically, I look at myself in the little square on the right side of

the screen and confirm that, indeed, this light would be great for recording a video on my beauty routine.

"In four weeks," I say.

"Four weeks? In three weeks it'll be late September already, and the client wants to see something now so they can close their budgets," replies another.

I feel like answering that I couldn't care less, as would any human being lucky enough to live off their ancestors' earnings; instead, I turn the pages of my notebook with great ceremony. I mumble, "Let me check a few things." I draw another tiny penis. "Give me two weeks," I finally say, and everyone is happy. The trick is to always offer a decoy date and then give them the one you had prepared in advance, like someone running a shell game or the way vendors at the Rastro flea market make you think you're getting a bargain.

We say goodbye with smiles and many thanks and a few calls of "Keep up the great work!" I log out of Zoom. My throat is so dry I can barely swallow. When I see my lonely reflection on the screen, I think again of Marina Joyce. If someone had turned up the volume during our call, they too would've heard a little voice saying "help me" and would've called the police.

I'm thirty-two, and I've been working in advertising for eight years, the last four at this agency. I started out as an intern, then they hired me as a copywriter, and now I'm in a middle management position with employees working under me and an absurd English diploma that allows me to show off on LinkedIn and make small talk on Tinder. The truth is I don't know how to do anything and I don't know how I got here. I suppose it was by perfecting the office game until everybody believed I was a great professional.

My job is to be nice and sell snake oil. I read the brief for a shitty product that's just like every other shitty product—a red lipstick; a perfume with floral notes; a vacuum cleaner with a tiny, triangular add-on that you can use on the corners of your house. Then I think about the nonsense that worries ordinary people, no matter how much they think they're the smartest sheep in the flock—being ugly, smelling bad at the end of the day, having a dirty house. The market generates needs, and it's my job to translate them into the language of ordinary mortals. I'm selling not red lipstick, but the idea of making an impact, of being beautiful, of leaving a mark on the collar of a handsome man's shirt. I'm not selling a perfume, but the idea of being remembered for your smell, of leaving an impression, of not being a gray, boring person who spends two hours of their life every day getting to and from work. I sell the possibility that today, yes, today, with the help of that floral perfume, something extraordinary will happen to you. I'm not selling the umpteenth vacuum cleaner that no one needs; I'm selling the idea of having a nice, clean house, of being able to take a photo of that cute little corner you decorated Pinterest-style, uploading it on Instagram, and getting a lot of likes. Then I pitch a creative idea that's like all the other creative ideas, the ones that came before and the ones that will come afterward. The lipstick effect. The smell of memories. Your dream house. They buy my idea, they pay us, I get congratulated, and we start all over again.

I've been doing the same thing for eight years, and I know it doesn't help anyone. I know the world would be a better place if jobs like mine didn't exist. I know I take advantage of people's insecurities and their desire to thrive in a society where no one can improve. And I know this because even I, after an eight-hour day full of elevator conversations that drive me to low-stakes suicidal ideation (like stapling my hand to get out of a meeting that makes me understand the true meaning of the word "infinite," or pouring boiling water from the office kettle onto myself so I can spend five to ten days at home with my feet up), still believe that the solution to all my problems will be a floral Zara dress made in Bangladesh that has followed me on every website I've visited today, and that, in all certainty, will be worn by millions of women on the street next season. I still believe that dress will turn me into a different woman, a happy, carefree, springtime version of myself. I know that when you buy something, what you're paying for is the promise of a better life. I know I'm also taking advantage of and accepting money from mediocre clients who think the greatest act of creativity is adding one more row to an Excel spreadsheet.

My work is measured by something as vague as its "impact." "Impact" can mean making something go viral. Or creating a catchy tune. Or winning one of those prestigious advertising awards that only matter to advertisers and the client who spent a fortune on some ad with a model who just really wants a hamburger and a hug. OK, if you're in every metro station in the city, it might be more likely that people will ask for your product at the perfume counters in the Corte Inglés department stores, but I don't think "The scent of memories" has a greater impact on their purchasing decisions than "A scent to remember." I'm good at selling ideas to clients. I make them believe they're unique, their product is wonderful, and this campaign will make a difference. I suck up to them, laugh at their jokes, flirt with them. My clients work for brands that don't want to take risks because they don't have to. When they take a stance on something, it's because everyone else already has, and therefore they feel it's safe to do so. Feminism, sustainability, inclusion, diversity . . . bullshit. Some brand hawking anti-cellulite and anti-aging creams wants to get away from the negativity associated with its product and empower women. So the campaign's approach will no longer be to make women think they're old or fat and they *need* a cream, but that they *deserve* that cream no matter how they look.

I turn the air-conditioning on full blast in the meeting room and write an email to the advertising students I'll have that fall in the master's program at a private university that hired me thanks to the English diploma I listed on LinkedIn.

Dear future students:

In order to establish some organizational parameters for the course we'll begin in September, I would like to give you an experimental assignment intended to gauge the skills of the class and establish our teamwork methodology.

The assignment is as follows: Think about how you would organize a large cosmetics company's Christmas campaign. I want you to think about both strategy (campaign launch times, deadlines, timing, calendar approach, etc.) and specific creative ideas for four types of products: perfume, lipstick, skin care product for 40+ women, and an eye shadow kit. The deadline for this exercise is three days from now.

Thank you all.

I walk to the water tank, fill up one of the tiny cups, and drink as I look out on the Gran Vía. I imagine the students happily believing this "assignment" will give them an opportunity to make an impression. They are fresh out of college and full of enthusiasm and joie de vivre. Their parents have the money to pay for a master's degree that will get them an unpaid internship at an agency where they'll end up staying. They have the money to buy their children employment, to give them access to prospective jobs others can't reach. In less than a week, they will send me their ideas; I'll choose the best ones and bring them to my team so they can develop them and put together a presentation. In the years I've been in advertising, I have also mastered the art of working as little as possible. Offices are like hunting—the more you move, the less chance you have of being shot.

I fill up another little cup before leaving the meeting room. My office is full of plastic cups. I often throw them in the bin at night and then take the bag out myself, to make sure no one thinks I hate dolphins. There are so many little cups that I could build a fort with them. I vaguely remember that not long ago, perhaps last Christmas, the company gave us a reusable water bottle out of their "commitment to sustainability." Right now, it's 62 degrees inside the office, while the street thermometer reads 100.

The office is almost empty in August. With those on vacation and those working remotely from nicer places, sometimes I feel like the only person left in Madrid. But I like that feeling. I enjoy August in the city because there's no one outside.

I stop at Natalia's desk before entering my office. Natalia—perfect blond hair in a long bob, polka-dot Zara dress, marked-up notepad, pens and highlighters in all the colors of the rainbow. Efficient, neat, always available as a means of compensating for her (completely justified) fear of not being a brilliant enough copywriter. One hundred percent company person. Natalia always wants to impress and be liked by me, and every time I stand in front of her, she looks up at me with her little eyes full of light and hope. She is always waiting for her big break, and I'm always willing to give it to her. She sends me emails at eight in the evening that I almost never respond to. She is here when I arrive in the morning and stays "a little bit longer" after I leave.

"Do you have five minutes?" I ask, knowing she's going to say yes. Natalia would give me the rest of her life if I asked her to.

"Of course."

"I need a few things for the Christmas campaign. Some market insights—how consumers will behave this Christmas, who has the most purchasing power, what products will generate the most interest." I'm already bored by what I'm saying.

Natalia writes everything down. I know she'll tell her friends how much she's learning and how much she loves her job. She's one of those people who will never consider whether spending countless hours a day at work is a waste of time and energy. She will continue enjoying her days at the office, the company culture, the after-work drinks on Thursdays and the beers on Fridays. She will take to heart all those "Find a job you love and you'll never have to work again" slogans. Her best friend will end up being Sonsoles from HR. She will get married, have children, buy a small apartment in a residential development on the outskirts, perhaps close to the airport, with a swimming pool. She will get together on weekends with friends who will also have children and live in residential developments with swimming pools, perhaps even in the same one, and she will feel like the special one at every dinner because she has a creative job. I know she will be immensely happy with that kind of life, and that gives me mixed feelings—pity, a pang of envy, and an almost uncontrollable desire to slap her.

"OK," she says as she writes.

"I also need you to start putting together the presentation. When is everybody back from vacation?"

"Luis and Claudio will be back next week, Marta in two weeks."

"Well, can you do it all?"

"I think so."

"Thank you, Natalia. That way I can focus on other stuff," I say vaguely, and turn on my heel toward my office.

My office is a glass cubicle with views of the entire floor. It looks like every advertising manager's office—a wooden table with a Day-Glo-painted Greek sculpture on it, a Nordic-style chair, two plants in a corner (a bird-of-paradise and a monstera),

and an imitation fifties locker. Now it's fashionable for middle
managers and bosses not to have their own office; for them to
be outside, with the rabble, as if we're all equal, although some
are on minimum wage while others are making up to 100,000
euros a year. Open spaces, huge rooms, and an absolute lack of
privacy are all the rage. I rejected the restructuring of my floor
by voting against it in an email survey, claiming that having an
enclosed private space helped the creative process, "as Virginia
Woolf already pointed out in *A Room of One's Own*," subtly
introducing the idea that being out in the open was somehow
misogynistic, when the truth was that a separate office gave me
the privacy to watch my YouTube videos.

I just love YouTube. I love every corner of it. I can start
watching videos of dogs that say words when they bark and
end up watching a video about how George Soros finances
entire global media conglomerates. I love conspiracy theories,
beefs between YouTubers, cultural wars. I love philosophical
or sociological explanations of the world. I love BookTubers.
I love twenty-minute-long compilations of children falling,
people who sing badly in singing competitions, or women who
try to follow makeup tutorials but somehow end up without
eyebrows. I love YouTubers who explain why we must free
Britney Spears from the clutches of her father. Or funny mon-
tages where the latest stupid thing a politician said is played
against techno music. I love tutorials. I can spend hours watching videos about how to apply crazy makeup that I will never
try myself, or recipes I'll never cook, or ways to organize small
spaces in the house I'll never own, or pelvic floor exercises you
can do while working, even though I'll never do them while I
work. I explore the catacombs of YouTube, searching for videos
of people smashing their faces into bread, or eating live octo-
puses in Japan and choking on them, or claiming they found
Hitler in Fuerteventura. But, without a doubt, my favorite
videos, the ones that transport me, are the ones about how

things are made. And I don't mean practical things like how to make a table or a chair, but rather how candy is made, how a potato chip factory works, how screws are made, or how pieces of marble are cut into compact blocks. YouTube is my window into a world I wish I could never leave.

I log into my account, and YouTube shows a series of videos that might interest me. I'm interested in all of them. Just as I'm about to click on one that will send me right into the modern world's rabbit hole, my office phone rings. I pick it up while still staring at the screen. Work wants to intrude on my window into the world. One of the girls in charge of the client's account forgot to tell me that the client also wanted ideas for an eyelash curler, although it's not the most important campaign item. "Think PARTY," she tells me. I say I'll work on it, but that I need more information about the product, as if I had spent my entire life underground, living in the sewers. I hang up.

I play a video of a failed proposal: An American guy wants to ask his girlfriend to marry him, but he's looking to do something special. The guy, whose girlfriend apparently "loves musicals," decides to orchestrate a flash mob in a mall on a random afternoon. Come D-Day, while he and his girl are walking around looking for something uninspiring, the boyfriend, the customers, and some of the workers begin to dance in the concourse around a mock-Renaissance-style fountain. The song is that horror titled "Happy," by Pharrell Williams. The woman, who can't understand what's happening, is stunned when he kneels on the ground and takes a ring out of his pocket. She rejects him in front of the fountain and a hundred people. The guy ends up crying and explains that he couldn't imagine she would turn him down in front of a crowd, but that he's decided to upload the video anyway in case he can "help other people." Protected by the internet's anonymity, I go to the comments section and write from one of my three accounts: "Hello? Is this 911? Please send this man a boo-hoombulance." I stay a few minutes to watch the likes increase and emojis of faces crying with laughter appear under my comment. The number quickly reaches twelve. I feel the slight rush I imagine addicts feel after a good fix.

I look away with a victorious smile that disappears as soon as I see my reflection in the windowpane. I'm wondering if I should spend the rest of the morning leaving rabid comments on YouTube videos, or if maybe I should do something with my life. I check my calendar and realize I don't have any more meetings today. Blessed August. It's too nice outside to spend the entire day watching YouTube. I tell Natalia I'm going to a meeting with some clients, and if she needs me she should send an email and only call if it's an emergency. But I know she won't call me for the rest of the day because she's terrified of bothering me with something stupid, and she's terrified of bothering me with something stupid because, every time she writes to me outside of working hours, I make an effort to respond in a laconic and curt way, so little by little I have been training her as if she were a Pavlovian dog that I only allow to drool on my shoes when we're in this glass cage we call "office."

I go out and take a taxi to the Prado Museum.

II

The Prado Museum is my favorite place in Madrid, along with the Quevedo 24/7 Carrefour market. Both are spacious, clean, tidy, and have air-conditioning. Between the two of them, they have everything I can ask for in life—one nourishes my body; the other nourishes my soul.

When I was eighteen and studying art history, my dream was to work at the Prado Museum, because I imagined nothing bad could happen when you're surrounded by beautiful things. After graduation, armed with my brand-new degree and convinced that Spain would never fall apart, I met a crazy advertising guy in a nightclub and he hired me for his agency, because back then those were the crazy things crazy advertising people did after having a bowl of cocaine for breakfast. The trend, back when there was money, was to hire advertising graduates as interns and then add a couple of people with different profiles, with no experience in the field, to provide "freshness," "new ideas," and "diverging visions." My cohort of interns included two advertising students, a taciturn musician who quit after a week, and me.

The job wasn't complicated—I attended meetings, took notes

and transcribed them, contributed ideas when they asked my opinion, spruced up the PowerPoints, and stayed to help with important deadlines, even if my help consisted of ordering the pizzas for dinner. I guess I thought it would be temporary, that life would lead to something else, that at some point I would escape from there. Or I thought this job would at least help me earn enough money so that I could devote my evenings to my true, indeterminate, artistic vocation. All my college classmates had started getting jobs and building their lives and talking about their new jobs and how they were building their lives. I think I got carried away. A year later, the agency gave me my first contract as a human rather than an intern. Now that I had a salary, I decided to stay a little longer. But because everyone was still traumatized after the 2008 crisis, I kept hearing how lucky I was to have a job, and I suppose we were all afraid to quit and pursue our dreams and, in my case, the advertising world seemed safer and more reliable than the hypothetical and increasingly distant world of art. I guess I made the wrong decision. Or maybe, between the possibility of being happier and buying more things, I chose to buy more things.

I show my Friend of the Museum card and enter. I go to the bathroom to pee and look in my bag for something to make my visit more enjoyable. I take out my Ativan blister pack and put a pill under my tongue. I leave the stall and drink water straight from the sink. Soon my bones feel like they have become the bones of a bird, hollow and weightless. I experience that feeling Pilates teachers always describe— that an invisible rope is pulling me upward, raising me above everything and everyone, everything that matters but also everything that doesn't. I feel slightly lightheaded, but it's the equivalent of two glasses of wine and not a whole bottle. It's such a familiar lightheadedness that a part of me has begun to recognize it as home. I leave the bathroom and walk slowly, keeping my back straight, rising above everyone else. It feels like my feet are sliding along one of those airport conveyor belts. There is no better place than the Prado Museum or the Quevedo 24/7 Carrefour. I pretend to be deciding what to see today, but I already know my body is asking for Hieronymus Bosch. I feel Hieronymus Bosch understands me; I feel he has the same demons as me, except he was a painting genius capable of exorcising them with his fingers and his brush, while I need Ativan and YouTube videos.

A few years ago, I decided to go to therapy after I started having anxiety attacks every time the alarm clock went off—the morning *beeeep* always produced an oppressive feeling in my chest. Not every morning was the same—sometimes it felt like I had a small chickpea lodged somewhere in my sternum, and other times as if an invisible hand was squeezing my heart. It became so ubiquitous that I learned to live with it. I even named it—I called it Berto, after my first high school boyfriend, a blond, skinny boy I started dating because he looked like Aaron Carter.

Little by little, that black hole drew my entire being toward it, increasingly darkening my days. Berto almost always arrived accompanied by crying. Not just any crying, but an agitated and ceremonious weeping, the inconsolable weeping of small children looking for their mother in the supermarket and of recent widows who chance upon their deceased husband's metro pass. Berto and crying became routine, something so customary that I sometimes cried in the shower to save time because I couldn't afford another day of being late for work. The alarm clock wasn't the only thing capable of opening the floodgates—in the office, sometimes my internal sirens would sound when I was caught off guard by the microwave beeping or the alarm on a motorcycle blaring outside the building. More than once, when the clock I'd set so nap time wouldn't get out of hand beeped, I would leap out of bed and get dressed for work, until I realized it was the weekend and I didn't have to go. Then a disproportionate joy invaded me, a joy that didn't fit in my chest, the joy of lost children when they finally find their mother or of widows when they discover yoga.

One morning I was grabbing a disgusting, watery take-away coffee from the cafeteria when my heart began beating faster and faster. I felt dizzy and had to look for something to lean on. Rita was with me, so I held on to her for fear of collapsing in the middle of the cafeteria. Rita was a graphic designer from my department. We'd been sharing a workspace for a year and a half; she was fascinated by Russian literature, as I discovered one day when, I don't know why, we ended up sitting in front of each other at the break room's communal table, each with a book—mine, *Strangers on a Train*; hers, *The Gambler*—and a packed lunch—mine, pasta salad, tuna, and hard-boiled egg; hers, pasta salad, tuna, and hard-boiled egg. We were surrounded by colleagues who used their lunch break to talk about work.

I didn't know Rita well, and her presence didn't attract much attention, since she was often so silent that it took a while to realize she was there, like that morning in the cafeteria. But we'd had a series of encounters that could be classified as pleasant. The most important one had been that day in the break room, when we realized we were both carrying books as shields so no one would sit with us and talk about advertising campaigns and PowerPoints. We both thought doing that made us different from the rest, but it was actually nice to see that wasn't the case.

To this day, I still don't know why I answered "no" when she asked me, "Marisa, are you OK?" but I'm glad I did. Maybe it was because Rita used to sigh like a Victorian lady when someone said something stupid in a meeting, because she didn't mind showing our colleagues that she was there not out of choice, but obligation. Or perhaps it was because we had both discovered, after a year-end performance presentation, that we couldn't stand the way Maika, the commercial director, spoke in a tone that made you feel like you were a waitress at a five-star hotel in an underdeveloped country. Since that day in the break room, we greeted each other every morning with what seemed like a sincere and not simply protocol smile, and from time to time, we made incisive and ironic comments in meetings that were clearly directed at each other, like two cautious lovers who can't make their relationship public. That day was one of the rare moments I spoke the truth to one of my coworkers and, sitting in the large cafeteria as our coffee got cold inside cardboard cups, I was honest with her about the episodes I'd been experiencing for months.

"Marisa, that's anxiety—you know that, right?"

I shook my head. I didn't know. I thought anxiety was a series of very specific symptoms (sweating, palpitations, a feeling of suffocation). Not bursting into tears when the alarm beeped and naming that feeling after the boy who'd called you a "cock tease" in high school.

"You need to go to the doctor; it can have very serious consequences. Make an appointment using the company's health insurance and have it looked at."

For some reason, I listened to Rita. I made an appointment with a general practitioner, an older man who took my blood pressure while asking me if I had been sexually abused as a child. I told him about the stress of going to work, and he prescribed me tranquilizers for the first time and recommended I start therapy.

What neither that doctor nor the therapist understood was that the stress was caused not by what I did at my job but, as I'd tried to explain to him, by having to go to work. Spending eight hours from Monday to Friday on alienating and unsatisfying tasks, surrounded by people with whom I was forced to have futile and boring conversations full of absurd platitudes about mortgages or parking spaces or the words their children said wrong or the last series they'd watched on Netflix. All that time I was giving to others instead of staying at home reading or drawing or simply looking at the ceiling, half naked, observing the cracks. I couldn't stand the idea of being forced to live that office pantomime in perpetuity just to pay for things like rent or food or a book or a weekend at the beach. I broke down every morning when the alarm beeped because life, lived this way, seemed like a badly written tragedy, boring and sterile, devoid of fun and, even worse, devoid of content, and so, on my way to work, I felt like grabbing strangers by the shoulders and asking them why they weren't feeling like me. What was their secret, how did they manage to maintain their composure, why didn't they cry every time their alarms beeped? And the truth is that before going to the doctor and the therapist, I already knew what my problem was, and also that, unless I won the lottery or cut off my hand so I could receive a state pension instead of working, my situation was hopeless. Therefore, since there was no way out of the system, and I could only hope to get through it without crying in the shower, I stopped going to therapy but continued accepting the tranquilizers. I pick them up from the same general practitioner, who gives them to me without asking too many questions because I told him that, in fact, I had been sexually abused as a child.

Hieronymus Bosch is the closest thing I have now to going to therapy. His work is strategically placed for highest drama: down in the depths of the museum, entering the world of shadows, you walk through dimly lit rooms until his paintings are revealed in all their splendor. The crown jewel, his *Garden of Earthly Delights* triptych, includes three panels more than two meters high that invite you to lose yourself in their details and discover things you'd never noticed before. Hieronymus Bosch's life is fascinating because he was a solitary man who almost never left Den Bosch, the Dutch city where he was born. Every time I approach the triptych, I'm reminded of how imposing and terrifying that Dutchman's inner world must have been for him to have barely seen anything or interacted with anyone in the outer world. I stand once again stunned in front of the work, and the cold air-conditioning makes my skin crawl.

The *Garden of Earthly Delights* triptych is three universes in one. The first panel represents the Garden of Eden on the last day of Creation, with Adam and Eve being blessed by a God who has granted them everything—fruit trees; rivers and lakes; animals of all kinds, from giraffes to elephants, birds and bears, even a unicorn. However, the devil appears in the ponds and on the rocks, lurking, waiting to tempt its two inhabitants. It's like the electric calm you feel in the air before a big storm—the garden seems like paradise, but a few disconcerting elements announce that something bad is about to happen.

The second universe, which gives its name to the work and immediately draws attention, is the "garden of earthly delights" itself, where humanity has succumbed to sin and is heading toward perdition. My theory is that Hieronymus Bosch, a pious man who lived according to the teachings of his local church, masturbated in the face of humanity with this work. *The Garden of Earthly Delights* is the 1500s' Pornhub. It's everything no one admits they do, feel, or look at, put onto oak panels—naked men and women everywhere, of different races, united by their sexual organs. There is heterosexual and homosexual sex; there is interracial sex; there is anal, oral, and vaginal sex; there is masturbation. Humans fuck, animals fuck, plants fuck. Everything you see that seems not to be sex is also sex—cherries, strawberries, apples and grapes, robins and crows, mussels and shells, leopards and deer. The garden of earthly delights is vibrant and voluptuous, colorful, passionate, and endless. It's that party where the music never stops, that restaurant where there's always another dish about to arrive, that movie where something happens after the credits.

That's why I don't want to move on to the third panel—it's

too early to descend into hell. I take a few steps back to see it in all its magnitude. I think about how little meaning life has, about the ephemeralness of pleasure, about those few moments of full bliss and enjoyment we find in our daily lives, before the string of more vulgar concerns pounces on us: the boiler inspection, the unanswered email in my inbox, the meeting next week. I think of guilt always lurking, of the alarm clock telling us it's time to do other things, of abrupt goodbyes, of rushing to the bus, of stomach cramps. And, suddenly, as if lightning had struck my brain, facilitating new, lucid, and strange connections, I think that Hieronymus Bosch was not condemning humanity with this garden, nor warning us of what would happen if we lived in sin, but rather he was showing everything desirable, everything possible, everything magnificent that life and the world could offer—a diverse and kind place, free of guilt and pain, where humans and animals coexist with nature and devote themselves in body, mind, and soul to the exploration of pleasures.

I gulp. I'm not capable of directing my gaze toward hell because I already spend too much time in it. Today I feel in communion with the garden. I feel like I'm the only person in the entire museum who can understand what Hieronymus Bosch meant. I put my hand on my chest. My blood pressure is at rock bottom, and since I don't want to faint, I say goodbye to Hieronymus Bosch in silent gratitude and take a taxi home.

III

At home, I turn on the air-conditioning, drink a glass of water, and sit in the living room with my laptop on my legs. I have six work emails. Four of them are students from the master's program with questions about the exercise. I can sense they're only asking to show me they are serious, intelligent, and well prepared, in order to win me over before the course starts. One of them asks for more of a brief. "There isn't any," I respond. Another asks what media the campaign is directed at. "Think big," I respond. The other two mostly want to introduce themselves and get my attention because they never actually formulate a concrete question, so I ignore them.

I have another email from the girl in accounts who'd promised to send more information about the eyelash curler: "It's a molding curler that lets you have easy, quick Hollywood-style lashes in your own bathroom." I abstain from asking why anyone would want to have Hollywood-style lashes in their own bathroom and just answer with a friendly "Thanks a lot!"

The last email is from my company's CEO. Subject: "Team-building retreat: this is what you've been waiting for. 😛" Cold sweat runs down my back. This weekend all the executives and mid-level management have to attend team-building work sessions outside the office. They've been meting out the information with an eyedropper. All we know is that we're leaving on Friday morning and coming back Saturday afternoon. Team building is another one of those idiotic ideas that American companies trying to imitate Google started. Group sessions, motivational pep talks, team games, and outdoor exercises aimed to have all the employees work shoulder to shoulder and, when it's over, for them to be more united and motivated to work harder when they return. "Teamwork makes the dream work." The company as family. The idea that your coworkers are more than coworkers, so the last thing you want to do is leave the office at six p.m. because you feel like you're abandoning your little brother at a gas station.

Since I have no kids or ailing parents, and I was too lazy to invent some rare disease, I have to go. The company's been planning it for months. The idea of spending a weekend with people from my office is about as appealing as ripping out my toenails. Every message from the CEO is more horrible than the one before: first he confirmed the dates, later he told us we should bring comfortable clothes and comfortable shoes, then he said we should bring a swimsuit. It's like we're gradually agreeing to the terms of our own kidnapping.

I open the new message and find that our destination is finally revealed: a five-star hotel in the middle of nowhere, in Segovia, surrounded by nature and with a spa, the cherry on top. The plan is to leave Madrid in a bus around eight in the morning and do a "team-building exercise" before we even drop our luggage. In the evening, we'll have "two very special speakers," and then we'll enjoy each other's company in "a relaxed environment" so we can "speak with self-criticism and empathy about the company and how we can improve within it." He says there are more surprises to come.

I want to vomit. I try to recover the feeling I had in the Prado, rescue Hieronymus Bosch from the depths of my brain to lift my mood and energy levels, but I can't find him anywhere. Bosch is off somewhere fucking a hydrangea, and I'm checking my work email. I wonder if I should call my trusted dealer, since the weekend's coming up. At first I thought that a couple of joints would be plenty. Now that I have more perspective, MDMA would be better. I put a reminder in my phone to call him and I close my inbox, where replies are starting to pile up. "I can't wait for this, guys!" "I'm so stoked." "We're going to have a total blast."

I feel around in my purse and stick another Ativan under my tongue. I don't understand why my coworkers are excited, if, in fact, that avalanche of emojis and exclamation points really translates into excitement and not that one of them, on the other side of the keyboard, is having a brain hemorrhage. I can't comprehend why they'd want to spend more time with colleagues rather than with their families, their friends, their hookups, or alone. Maybe they're terrified of that last option. Or perhaps they're faking it too, for Lord only knows what reasons. For a potential promotion or for the warm sensation of a little pat on the back from the company's top brass. I put my laptop on the kitchen table and go out onto the terrace.

I live in a small apartment: thirty-five square meters in the Chamberí neighborhood, with another ten square meters of terrace. The apartment has a living room, a bedroom, a small separate kitchen, and a bathroom. I chose it because of the terrace. I've always liked terraces. My terrace is where I spend most of my time, except when it's unbearably hot or cold. In my ideal world, buildings in big cities would be built like pyramids so that we could all have a terrace with plants draping down onto the terraces below. I think everyone deserves a patch of sky. When I could still read, I read a lot. Now every time I pick up a book, I get through the first paragraph, then switch to literary analyses on YouTube. I can't remember the passages I used to love, but sometimes phrases come to me, like flashes from a previous life. Whenever I'm on the terrace, out of sight and with my mind blank, I think about something I read somewhere I can't recall, that said something like this: "I have every useless thing in the world in my house there. The only thing wanting is the necessary thing, a great patch of open sky like this. Always try to keep a patch of sky above your life . . ." It's true that we all deserve a slice of sky above our lives; otherwise it's all just asphalt and stucco.

My cell phone vibrates. It's 5:30. I've tricked capitalism for one more day, and I don't have to put back on that constricting, uncomfortable disguise again until tomorrow morning. I open WhatsApp and discover the vibration was a note from my neighbor Pablo. He asks if I want to hang out later. Pablo and I have been sleeping together ever since he moved to the third floor five years ago. Our sexual relations are intermittent and our romantic relationship nonexistent, but our friendship is unbreakable. Pablo and I only work as a pseudo-couple inside the safe walls of our respective homes and beneath the sky of my terrace. He's had a couple of serious girlfriends in those five years and I had a steady relationship for a few months, and we never had sex then. Now he's single and so am I, and once in a while, he comes up to my place, and we drink, talk for hours, and sleep together. I run my hand over my legs. "I'll let you know later," I reply. I'd have to shave first.

Sometimes masturbating is more practical. I'm not always in the mood to talk, listen, pay attention, sit up straight, and comb my hair. Not devoting even a smidgen of attention and affection to the person you're about to go to bed with feels disrespectful. Other times I have a powerful need for attention and affection: I need to talk and be listened to, to be touched and held, for someone to look into my eyes, to desire and be desired, to live the fantasy—for a few moments—of the nice parts of being in a relationship. Everything's easy with Pablo and, occasionally, the lie feels real. Sometimes I wish we could fall in love with each other, but we both know full well that if it hasn't happened yet, it's never going to. "OK, I'll be at home," I follow up. I think it was Julian Barnes, or maybe some other British guy, who had a pretty dead-on definition of love being like a scowl suddenly relaxing. When I'm with Pablo, I feel my facial muscles easing, but when I say goodbye and close the door, they always go back to their natural state of tension.

I enter my apartment and close the door to the terrace. It's too hot. I go to the fridge and pull out some leftover potato salad. I eat it standing up, leaning on the kitchen counter with a fork trying not to think about how sad it is to eat leaning on the kitchen counter with a fork. I drink two glasses of water and stretch out on my bed. I open YouTube, put on an ASMR video, and fall into a deep sleep listening to a woman whisper articles from the Spanish Constitution.

When I wake up, it's a quarter to nine. YouTube has been choosing videos of its own volition, and now on the screen is an old political program from Channel 2 where four gray-haired men are discussing the Transition to democracy. Surely they must be dead by now, but here, in my bedroom, they are not only alive but arguing loudly. I think how the internet is a magical place with the power to revive the dead. I stretch and turn the video off. Perhaps because I was sweating in my sleep, or because of the feel of the sheets between my legs, it seems like a good idea to have some company tonight. I write to Pablo and tell him that I could have a glass of wine in half an hour.

"Do you want to come down or should I come up?" he answers.

"Come up, I'll jump in the shower."

I get beneath the stream of water and rub soap all over my body; then I run the razor over my legs very carefully, dividing them into zones like parcels of land in the countryside. I go over those lands again and again so not a single wayward hair remains. Over the course of my life, I've read Simone de Beauvoir, Betty Friedan, Virginia Woolf, Kate Millett, Silvia Federici, Angela Davis, Judith Butler, Virginie Despentes. None of that matters. I still shave every other day, even when there isn't a single human in all of Madrid who has even the slightest possibility of seeing my armpits. I still can't stand the sight of a single hair anywhere that I don't want it to be. At my job, for a whole string of shitty brands, I send out empowering messages to women I'll never meet telling them to stop feeling bad about their stretch marks, varicose veins, wrinkles, spare tires, and cellulitis, yet, ever since I've started making money, I buy the most expensive creams and cosmetics that promise the best results for my stretch marks, my wrinkles, my flaccid flesh, and my cellulitis.

I frequently examine myself in front of the mirror, worrying that if I ever see wrinkles, I'll begin smiling less to stay looking younger a little longer. On Instagram, I "like" reels of women showing off their fat rolls in their bedrooms. I apply a strong cold massage cream that promises to burn fat on my thighs while I sleep for just 78 euros. I share threads on Twitter about the need to free ourselves from the patriarchal canons of beauty. I fast for two days before going to the beach so my stomach will be flat. I shout at some random guy who says something dirty to me when I'm walking down the street; I shout all the things I've been carrying around since forever, as if that guy represents every man who's ever catcalled a woman, and passing women smile with complicity ("You tell him, sister"), but, back at home, I realize that at just thirty-two years old, I haven't been catcalled on the street in a while. They save them for the younger girls, who don't have as much experience and the tools to defend themselves, who are more docile and shy and also have firmer breasts and higher glutes. I think that at fifteen, I heard nasty shit from them every day and I came home wanting to cry, and now a part of me wants to cry because they don't say anything. I think about the smoothness that Pablo will feel when he lays a hand on my leg tonight, and I rinse my hair and try to convince myself that I do all this not for other people but for myself, so I don't feel like a bad feminist in my steamy bathroom.

I towel-dry and untangle my hair. My body dries in the time it takes me to get from the bathroom to the bedroom. I love August. I put on black panties and a short black dress with spaghetti straps, and I go to the kitchen to uncork a bottle of wine. I feel totally gorgeous: clean and perfumed, exfoliated, smooth, without a single extra hair. Splendorous as a white swan. Pablo shows up right on time, with his characteristic three knocks.

"Are you feeling sick?" he asks as soon as I open the door.

"What?" I respond, disconcerted. The swan turns into a duck.

"I don't know, you look tired or something," he says as he makes himself at home, pulling a baguette, a cheese plate, and some potato chips out of a bag. "I mean, you look pretty, but your face is like death warmed over."

"Is this how the kids are picking up girls these days? Is that a neg?"

"A what?" Pablo pulls two wineglasses out of the cabinet. He knows where everything is, which creates a feeling of intimacy between us that is usually only shared by old married couples who finish each other's sentences.

"Do you know what a pickup artist is? The science of seduction?"

"Enlighten me, please."

I pour the wine into our glasses and we go out on the terrace. We always do the same thing. On cold days we sit in the living room, the rest of the time out on the terrace. It's nice not to have to tell a person where to sit and where the dishcloths are if some wine gets spilled. I guess that's what friendship is, the other person knowing exactly where all your things are, and how to solve the problems that arise without asking questions.

"Scientific seduction is a kind of self-help manual for men who don't know how to pick up women, wrapped in pseudo-science. Pickup artists are, like, teachers of that subject, and they give advice to a bunch of sheep who pay 300 euros each to try to learn how to talk to a woman." I take a sip of wine and observe Pablo. I don't think Pablo is someone who needs lessons on how to pick up women, but somehow, he belongs to the same species, the same genus. "The neg is one of the pickup techniques they teach, which consists of emotionally manipulating the person you're interested in. It's making a comment that seems positive but is actually negative, like, 'You're still hot, for your age,' or 'I think you look fantastic, I like girls with meat on their bones.' The woman lowers her guard, she gets flustered, because he hasn't said anything bad, but the comment has subtly lowered her self-esteem and, according to the theory, in order to recover it, she'll try to get the guy who made the comment to like her."

"Where do you get this crap from, Marisa?" asks Pablo, laughing. "Don't tell me: YouTube."

I nod with a slight smile. I can tell Pablo all the stories in the world, like Scheherazade, and I always have his interest and attention. Sometimes I think I spend hours watching YouTube so that I can talk about it later with someone like Pablo. The same way I sometimes think that Pablo comes up to my place just to hear someone like me talk.

"Yeah, it's a whole big thread. They teach psychological-abuse tactics to trick the kind of women who buy candles at Zara Home."

"Why Zara Home?"

"Because, Pablo, a woman buying candles at Zara Home is a woman on the verge of desperation."

Pablo spits out some of the wine he just drank and looks at me with amusement.

"And I negged you?" he asks, honestly surprised.

"Yes. You told me I'm pretty, but my face looks like death warmed over. It's a textbook neg."

Pablo stares at his glass, his brow furrowed. He is dark-haired, with chestnut-colored eyes and an aquiline nose, which makes him look a bit like a bird of prey, a cunning hawk.

"That's true. I'm sorry."

I smile. He definitely does not belong to the same species. Pablo has taken a small evolutionary step.

"No prob."

"You do look exhausted though."

I look up at the sky and let out an exaggerated sigh.

"It's true, what do you want me to say?" he asks.

"Don't say anything, Pablo, what need is there to speak your mind about other people's appearance? You don't see me going around saying you're wearing dad pants today."

"Dad pants?" He laughs and touches them.

They are khaki pirate cargo pants with more pockets than a person needs to survive the trek from the third to the fourth floor. They are the typical pants middle-aged men buy in bulk at stores like Decathlon, unaware that the basic rules of society dictate that no one should shop in a sportswear store if they don't play any sports. They are perfect pants for hiking or mountain climbing, but absurd for wearing around the city.

"That way I can carry all my stuff. Otherwise I don't know where to put it: there are no purses for men, and a fanny pack makes me look like a junkie parking valet."

"But how much stuff do you carry around?" I ask him. "A change of clothes in case you have an accident between the third floor and the fourth? Your family photo album in case your place burns down? For fuck's sake, you've got six pockets."

"I don't know, my keys, my phone, my wallet, a pack of cigarettes . . ."

"Come on, give me one."

Pablo stands up and pulls out the pack and a lighter; then he goes to the kitchen to get an ashtray and, in those few seconds, I realize that the city is incredibly silent. When Pablo gets back, I look at him with relief.

"Are you sleeping well? Are you eating well?" he asks.

I sigh again, looking up at the sky. I find his excessive concern for my well-being both amusing and exasperating, as if looking tired were a choice I'd made in the shower, while I shaved my legs and trimmed my bikini line.

"Yes, Daddy."

Pablo laughs, lights a cigarette, and passes it to me before lighting one for himself. For some reason, I find the gesture touching. Perhaps lighting a cancer stick for me isn't the healthiest example of what it means to care for someone, but it's not nothing either. I study the cigarette before taking a drag.

"But I have been really tired lately."

"Do you have a lot of work?"

"I don't know, it's not about my workload," I say as I adjust my back to relax. "It's like I fear the day's never going to end, even though it does, eventually. One day after the next and then the weekend and then it starts all over again. It's always the same day: I get up, shower, go to the office, come home, I make dinner and prepare my lunch for work the next day, take another shower, watch something on YouTube, and all of a sudden it's Wednesday or Thursday."

"Maybe you need a vacation, when's the last time you had a vacation?"

"Vacations are like putting a Band-Aid on an axe wound. You go to places where you'll never be able to live, to experience a lifestyle you can't afford, and then you come back and see on the news they're talking about 'post-vacation syndrome' when really what they should say is 'Your life is so horrible that you get depressed when you have to return after two weeks of fantasy.'"

Pablo listens and nods, but I don't know if he really understands. I should change the subject. I realize I'm stinking up the space with this droning torrent of common grievances.

"Whatever. How are *you* doing?"

"Good." Pablo takes a drag, then turns away from the cityscape to look at me. "I sometimes feel that way too, you know. Like everything's always the same and everything's always gonna be the same. Over and over again."

"And how do you shake that feeling?" I ask.

"Well, as you say, I'm a straight man, so I guess what I do is sweep all those feelings under the rug, put on a pair of pants with a lot of pockets, and ring you up for a booty call."

My laugh fills the silence of Madrid. I guess that's what we all do. Send those "howyoudoins" through WhatsApp, hoping our desperation, loneliness, and anguish aren't obvious, using a lot of exclamation points so they don't show. Those last-minute invitations for a beer or a glass of wine, when we feel like our ceiling's about to cave in and we're anxious for any sort of human contact. Those "Where you at?" DMs on Instagram to that friend group you haven't seen in months because exhaustion and sloth had gotten the best of you, but now all you need is a location and a "Come" so that the sound of a bar, the clinking of glasses and the babble of conversations, will drown out the growing shrill of your thoughts.

I take another swig of wine, another drag on my cigarette, make a couple of jokes, then direct the conversation toward something more blithe because we need to lighten that suffocating, sluggish August night in Madrid. I'm actively creating a memory for both of us. When we've each had three drinks, we obfuscate the rising volume of our conversation with an index finger caressing an arm. I can't remember whose arm it is, or whose finger, and by that point, it doesn't matter. Then we kiss in one of those carefully careless moments when one of us goes into the kitchen and the other decides to help out, and after that we kiss some more. The kisses lead us to the bed and in the bed we fuck. It's not an epic lay; it's a necessary lay. Some mutual relief, a gift we give each other, a way to end the night. Afterward we talk for a while with our eyes closed until we fall asleep. That night I don't need to search for something to watch on YouTube.

IV

When my alarm goes off, Pablo's already left. He's eliminated all traces of last night: the glasses are gleaming in the dish rack, the ashtray is empty, and there's a new bag in the trash can. I set into motion like a robot programmed for corporate life. I shower, drink a coffee, fix my face and hair, choose a flowing white linen dress and some sandals. I stick my laptop into my bag, wash the coffee mug, grab my lunch, and head to work.

It takes twenty minutes to walk to the office, and sometimes those minutes are the best part of my day. Rain, snow, or burning asphalt beneath my sandals, I always walk. Along the way, I think of hypothetical mishaps that would keep me from getting to the office. It's a matter of probabilities. I like to think that I might win the lottery, but it's much more likely I'll get run over by a bus. Recently I discovered that an accident on the way to work is considered an *in itinere* work accident, so you get paid your full salary while on leave, and ever since then, I cross the street carefree, sometimes even riskily. I step into the road as soon as the light turns green, hoping some imprudent driver will knock me down. A neck brace, a cast on my arm, medical leave from work, physical therapy, time for me. As usual, nothing happens. No driver runs me over, no cyclist crashes into me, no luck disguised as misfortune turns my day on its ear. But my mood doesn't tank when I cross through the glass doors of the building and I greet the doorman with a good-morning, because I still have the walk home.

I arrive at 9:15. Natalia is already at her desk and greets me with a wide, serene smile, as if she sleeps well at night. I smile back and enter my office. I go through my emails and calendar. I have a status meeting at ten with my boss, another meeting at eleven to see the brief on a new perfume, and another meeting at 12:15 to decide whether we are going to compete to represent a sports brand. I want to slit my wrists and it's not even 9:20. The office is almost empty, but my morning is full. I loathe the dynamics of meetings. I think some people enjoy them because they're a way to avoid working. I think other people use meetings as a self-love bath, to feel important. I can't stand the smorgasbord of clichés, the typical funny stories, the Anglicisms to try to add significance to the simplest procedures, the need to involve the pope and his mother in every minor project, or the tennis match that develops when someone wants to pass the buck and it gets lobbed right back.

I go for another coffee.

"You going for coffee?" asks Natalia. "I'll come with."

We walk in silence to the break room with a Nespresso machine and a little fridge. I pull two mugs from the cabinet. Mine has a childish drawing of a sun and the phrase "Today is gonna be a great day"; the one I give my coworker is bubble-gum pink and reads "Live more, worry less."

Natalia pulls two capsules from a drawer.

"Shit, this is unbelievable, they keep stealing my capsules."

I don't know whose life seems sadder, the office coffee capsule thief's or the person who experiences the coffee theft as persecution.

"Didn't the higher-ups send out a message?" I ask. "I think I got an email."

"Yeah, but, honestly, do you think those thieves are deterred by a message like that?" She says "those thieves" as if we're talking about organized crime, which both fascinates me and makes me want to slap her. "I was talking to my friends about it the other day, and in the end, we agreed that the company should put up security cameras."

"Security cameras to surveil coffee capsules." I grab my coffee and pour soy milk into it. "I don't know, Natalia, I don't see that happening."

"Today it's capsules, tomorrow it could be wallets. If there's a stealing problem in the office, the company should be prepared to put an end to it."

"I don't think there's a stealing problem in the office, I think someone needs their caffeine."

"So they should buy their own capsules! Isn't the company going to take a stand?"

I sip my coffee and close my eyes for a few seconds. I want to ask if she's considered how boring her life must be to make this into a whole big thing. I want to ask if all her friends have the same kind of first-world problems and if they're all as bored as she is. If none of them ever talks about the ménage à trois she had the other night with her husband and a stranger they chose on Tinder, or that after a few too many drinks she shat herself in the middle of the street, or that she's cheating on her boyfriend with a guy she met online in a forum about indoor plants. I also want to tell her that, instead of obsessing over shitty capsules, she could demand payment for all the overtime she puts in. Or worry about the interns' salaries, which are nonexistent, or the fact that our bosses routinely call us on our personal phones outside of office hours.

"Do you know how much it costs to set up a security camera?" I ask Natalia. Surprisingly I do because I recently watched a YouTube video about living in a society of hypervigilance. "At least 400 euros. The company isn't going to put a camera in the kitchen to find out who's robbing your coffee capsules because it would be cheaper to buy you a year's worth of coffee capsules, Natalia. And with the email they sent out, they feel they've done enough to solve a problem that, honestly, I don't think they're losing sleep over."

"Well, then you tell me," responds Natalia with her brow furrowed in annoyance.

"I will tell you: you can take your capsules to your desk and lock them in a drawer, for example."

"Ah, that's not a bad idea."

"Sure. Or you can type 'Smile, you're on camera,' into a Word doc, print it out, and tape it up right here. It's cheaper than installing a camera and probably has the same effect."

"But isn't that illegal?"

"I don't think it's illegal. You have my permission."

"Really?"

"Yeah."

"Thanks, Marisa." Natalia picks up her mug and heads to her desk with a spring in her step. A woman with a mission.

I finish my coffee in silence, drawing it out as I stare at the neutral-toned wall and imagine my walk back home. When I've finished, I put the mug in the dishwasher. Soon Julián from the design team shows up and grabs one of Natalia's capsules. I watch him out of the corner of my eye, trying to discern his dark motives. He doesn't seem like a thief, just clueless. Even if Natalia papered the walls with signs, Julián would never catch on.

"Hey, Marisa, didn't see you," he says, turning toward me. "Are you coming or going?"

"What?"

"Should I put a coffee on for you?"

"Oh. Yes, please." I smile and pull a new mug out of the cabinet. It reads "May all your wrinkles be laugh lines."

The ten o'clock meeting reminds me of a sporting competition. It's a race for who has the most work, with the prize being a gold star from their supervisor. Even though most of the team is on vacation and it's nearly 93 degrees outside and climbing, the low hum of August hasn't dampened the craving for a promotion or approval. My colleagues weigh in on old projects from past meetings just to get noticed; then they offer up new projects with excessive attention to detail to avoid criticism over delays, and they pressure people from other departments to send them things that are always incredibly urgent. "We need to know the results." "Can someone put together a report?" "Don't forget to copy me." "I have to hop on a call," saying the last word in English and pronouncing it like "coal." "Who's handling the talent?" "Send it to me on Slack later." "Kudos, great job!" "Thanks, now back to work." It's a perfumed jungle, baboons in suits, orangutans in high heels. If everyone realized how unimportant they actually were and how easily they could be replaced, they might be a bit nicer to each other.

I take a sip of my coffee. When my boss asks me what I'm working on, I feel too exhausted to answer, but I make an effort. I play the role, recite my pending tasks, pretend to have a ton of work to avoid getting some project dumped on me that cuts into my YouTube time. My boss seems satisfied. One more day cheating the system. The office game consists of knowing how to express yourself. To say "preparing an Excel" or "making a presentation" as if you were talking about open-heart surgery or to draw out an explanation with boring details so people lose the thread and don't ask questions when you've finished.

When the meeting's over, my boss asks me to stay behind for a couple of minutes.

"Marisa, I wanted to propose something to you for the team-building retreat."

"Sure, what is it," I respond, stifling a "No, please, no" with every fiber of my being.

"I'd like you to lead a creativity exercise for your coworkers, so that those who don't usually work on this side of things can better understand and value the work we do, since it's a bit more intangible. What do you think?"

"I don't know, Ramón, I've got a full plate already."

"Well, take some time off before the team-building retreat if you want."

"OK, Ramón, let's see what I can come up with," I say in fake modesty.

"I'm sure you'll do a fantastic job. I believe in you."

I leave the room with my mug of cold coffee and head toward my office. Ramón treats his employees like they're his teenage kids. He's constantly offering up motivational phrases like "I believe in you," "You can do hard things," and "I know you won't disappoint me." He's like a dad, a gray-haired man in a tie who pats us on the back and feels genuine pride when we do our job, but whose biggest weakness is that he can't bear to see anyone suffering and always tries to avoid conflict. It's easy to take advantage of his corporate kindness. I've seen colleagues who can't even open a Florette salad ask him if they can come in late every day to "take care of their children" and interns with hangovers that leave them gripping the doorframes asking to go home because of "an upset stomach." He won't give you a raise because it's "out of his hands," but he'll also never question that, even though last year two of your grandmothers died, this year another one did, and, as such, you need to take a few days off without running it by HR because he'll be too embarrassed to admit he'd assumed both your grandmothers were already dead.

Maybe I'll find some TED Talk on creativity I can plagiarize. "Marisa?"

I turn and see Ramón still in the doorway of the conference room. He seems vexed, possibly rheumatic. He approaches with a slow, labored gait, and he's frowning like he's trying to solve a complicated math problem.

"Ramón?" I say, walking over to him with the same halo of mystery.

Sometimes what's most important is imitation: If everyone seems worried, you should act worried; if everyone is happy, you should simulate happiness. If, as is the case now, it seems like a little boy's gotten stuck in the building's air ducts and nobody knows how to rescue him, you have to adopt the same concerned expression.

"On the team-building retreat . . ."

"Yes?"

"We don't want to give a bad impression."

"I understand," I say, not understanding.

"You know, with a frivolous or disrespectful image."

"Don't worry, I don't think giving a talk about creativity will make people think this is Sodom and Gomorrah."

"Of course. No. It's not that. I have complete faith in you, but . . ." He pauses, looks me in the eyes, and clears his throat. "After talking it over with human resources, we've decided we should have a minute of silence at some point over the weekend. For Rita."

First I notice the cold in my hands, as if I'd dunked them into a bucket of ice. Then the cold travels through my entire body. I look at Ramón, but his features blur. The hallway starts to seem unreal, narrower, more brightly lit, made of papier-mâché. The people walking in the background, from one side to the other, with notebooks and pens in their hands, suddenly seem like film extras who've been directed to wander around holding a fistful of blank pages behind the main characters. My hands start sweating. We are on some sort of set, shooting a movie. Interior/Day: I'm in an office. I'm wearing a white dress, gripping a cup of coffee and a notebook. I've come here to work. I swallow hard and press the button for the elevator. I stammer out a few words, a goodbye, an excuse. Something like "Yes, of course." Or a "That'd be fine." Or perhaps a "Good idea, see you later." I walk into the elevator and look at the pale, sweaty woman reflected in the mirror. I struggle to recognize that image as my own. I repeat to myself: My name is Marisa and I came here to work. I take a deep breath. I realize that it's three minutes to eleven and I have another meeting with Maika, from accounts, and one of her lackeys on the floor below. First I go up to the top floor and press all the buttons so I have more time to breathe deeply. My name is Marisa and I have a meeting at eleven o'clock. All that's required of me is that I go to that eleven o'clock meeting. People come in and out of the elevator. "Hi, Marisa!" Hi, Alfredo, Gustavo, Roberto, whoever you are. I breathe. I'm in an office. I came here to work. I take the name Rita and lock it in a drawer in the depths of my brain. It'll be fine there. I arrive at the floor of my meeting and exit the elevator decisively.

Sales teams are the same everywhere. Doesn't matter if you're an insurance salesman, real estate vulture, or work at a PR firm. Your job is selling and selling at any price. The more you sell, the more you earn. Your commission depends on how well you can kiss ass, how well you can lie, on the aggressiveness you use to put a client between the frying pan and the fire, and on the pressure you exert on your colleagues. All of that can get you a new purse, a bathroom redo, dinner at an expensive restaurant, and, of course, congratulations from your boss. Sales teams think in the short term; they want to see signatures and close deals. They make a show of fake sympathy, but their friendliness shatters as soon as something goes awry. They smile until they have what they want; then they're capable of calling you at any hour of the night screaming, of cornering you in a meeting room with five other people or sending you a passive-aggressive email with all your bosses copied. Hyenas. If I've learned anything in my years in this profession, it's that there's only one strategy to take with sales teams: smile and nod.

I enter the meeting room. Maika, head of accounts, just back from vacation, brown pantsuit and black heels, always wearing too much makeup and perfume, receives me with a smile. Estefi is calling in. I can't see her, but I sense her presence.

"Estefi, Marisa's arrived," explains Maika to the telephone, from which I intuit that a few seconds ago they were talking shit about me. "Marisa, how's it going? We're celebrating!"

"Hello, girlsss," I say. "What are we celebrating?"

"Estefi's pregnant!"

"OMG! Congratulations, Estefi!" I say into the phone.

"Thanks, sweetheart! I'm so happy!"

"Is it your first?" I ask, as if I care.

"Yes, I just came from the gynecologist and I can finally tell people, I've been dying to."

In offices, a pregnancy is always cause for celebration. Coworkers love to welcome a baby into the world. It's another excuse to make a toast, to say clichés, to carry out a ritual: a space where they feel comfortable. "Your life is going to change forever! But it's so worth it . . ." "Ay, the best decision of my life. There's nothing like it." "You'll see, it's pure joy." "Your mother must be thrilled, right?" "You can forget about getting any sleep!" "Is your husband practicing his diaper changing?" The ritual begins with the congratulations in *petit comité*, followed by an official congratulations in the monthly corporate email: "And last but not least! Our family is growing!" Then they organize a farewell toast before the future mommy or daddy goes on leave and, later, when the baby's been born, they collect money for a gift. Not long after, the new mother or father comes in to show off their newborn as if it were baby Jesus: they parade it around the office receiving congratulations and votes of confidence. A part of me wishes I would get pregnant so I could take maternity leave. Afterward, another cycle begins: the mommy returns and the joy evaporates. If she doesn't accomplish enough, she gets called out—now no one cares about her major life change and they just want her to get back to who she used to be, as soon as possible. If she asks for a shorter workday, it causes problems for everyone else. If she complains too much, maybe she wasn't cut out for this line of work. But if she doesn't complain at all, she's a weirdo who never talks about her kid. In an office, being a mother is a double-edged sword. A kid is always a joy, but a mother is a cog in the system, a cog that's starting to rust.

"I'm so happy for you, Estefi," I say.

As I've gotten older, I've noticed the widening gap between mothers and non-mothers. When you get to a certain age, not having children and not wanting them seems like an affront to the women who decide to have them. I'm aware that this is another tool of the patriarchy: divide and you shall conquer.

That said, I'm fed up with the mothers around me. The ones in my office become a portal to their babies. Through them, you learn every milestone in the infant's life, all explained in full detail, but which are actually completely run-of-the-mill: talking, walking, eating solid foods, gaining weight from one month to the next, not dying suddenly. Within this new dimension, Motherhood becomes the only religion and the New Moms are like missionaries in the colonial era. They spread their message of the benevolence of motherhood through the repetition of slogans: "This is the best thing that ever happened to me." "Sometimes I get stressed out, sure, but when I see my baby's little face, that makes it all better." "It doesn't get any better than this." "You realize that you didn't really know what love is." "Your old problems cease to matter." Having these women with dark circles down to their feet and more roots in their hair than a weeping willow talk to me about the perks of being a mother makes me distrust them. I don't understand why they want to sell me their product with such passion. There must be a catch.

"Thanks, sweetie," Estefi says.

We are meeting about a perfume launching this fall. It's the big launch of a popular cosmetics group, and they're expecting to rake it in at Christmastime. They're rebooting a classic perfume, one of the brand's first, which they're rescuing from oblivion in an attempt to position themselves as "timeless." They want a 360-degree campaign: television, radio, and digital.

"They're looking for a big WOW factor," says Maika.

Clients always say they're looking for a big WOW factor, but really that's the last thing they want. Especially when it comes to perfume, which has been sold the same way since forever: with a languid model in an elegant setting saying the name of the perfume in a French accent.

"When is this for?"

"We should start shooting in early October, so the proposal should be approved in mid-September at the latest," replies Estefi from the other side of the phone line.

"Great."

Estefi gives some vague guidelines before getting off the call. Maika makes sure the call has ended by picking up the receiver and replacing it on its holder three times.

"Can you believe her? Getting pregnant right before Christmas?" she says, staring at me, seeking out a possible ally in her open war against human rights.

"Shit, Maika . . ." I mutter as I gather my things.

"No, girl, you know what I mean, I'm happy for her, but if it turns into a complicated pregnancy, we're in for a hell of a ride. And even if it doesn't."

"Maika, you can't really say stuff like that."

I gave up years ago on the idea that everyone should agree with my moral principles. In the office I usually avoid controversial topics, and I ignore any veiled comments from colleagues seeking support for their murky ideologies. At this point, I'm satisfied if they don't spit out nonsense left and right, and if they do, I'd rather find out about it later, when someone tells me the gossip in the cafeteria.

"Why not? I'm just giving my opinion. I'm sick and tired of the PC dictatorship."

"Maika, come on, don't be a jackass."

Maika makes a surprised expression, and I do too. We stare at each other for a few seconds until I lower my gaze and gather up the rest of my things. It's as if I'd spilled a glass of water: it just happened, I didn't mean to express my opinion out loud, but I did, and now everything's soaking wet. I clear my throat, stand up, and look at her again.

"I'll send you the creative proposal sometime in the first week of September, if that sounds good to you."

"Perfect, Marisa, thanks a lot."

We say goodbye as if nothing had happened, ignoring the latent tension in favor of the sustained toxic positivity that usually reigns in the office. I leave the meeting room, fill up two little cups of water, and enter my office with my heart beating like crazy.

I don't know what happened or where it came from, but a crack has opened. My real opinions and feelings have no place here. That can't happen again. A song by the Smiths comes into my head, "Heaven Knows I'm Miserable Now." I search for it on Spotify and play it at a low volume while I stick a tranquilizer under my tongue.

I adore this song. I heard it for the first time on a bus from my internship to my waitress job. "I was looking for a job and then I found a job and heaven knows I'm miserable now." I don't remember how it came on shuffle; I do know that I got off at the next stop because the noise from the bus wasn't letting me listen to it carefully. Everyone believes that singers are speaking about them, especially love and breakup songs, but I recognized this song was about something else: the misgivings of the working class, the constant unhappiness despite meeting expectations; it was about doing what you think you should be doing and yet never feeling fulfilled. Morrissey was singing about the dissatisfaction caused by shit jobs and the obligation to pay bills, about the alienation provoked by hours at the office and little time to enjoy the true pleasures of life.

As I grew up and kept working, the song had a calming, healing effect on me, like singing Gregorian chants. I wasn't alone. There must be others like me, who faked contentment over small talk on the elevator, while inside they were falling into the void.

"In my life, why do I give valuable time to people who don't care if I live or die?" When I was still interning at the advertising agency, I worked on Thursday, Friday, and Saturday nights serving drinks at a bar downtown. One night I twisted my ankle on the way from one job to the other. I left the agency late because of a deadline that, as always, kept everyone in the office until it was time to order pizzas, and I was rushing to my shift at the bar. Running after a bus to take me downtown, I took a wrong step between the curb and the street and I fell to the ground. The doctor told me I had a sprain and should stay off it for a few days. When I called the bar, they asked me how many days exactly my staying off it entailed. When I called the agency, they told me I could work from home with my foot elevated. I didn't have a contract at the bar, and the agency paid just enough to cover my transportation costs. Nobody cared about my health; they only cared about when I was coming back to work and what I wasn't getting done until I did. They didn't care if I lived or died. If I were to die tomorrow, their main concern would be who was going to take over the Christmas campaign. As soon as I realized that most people at my job dehumanized me, it was easier to dehumanize them. I replay the song and observe my right ankle. Ever since that day, I have the feeling that it's fatter than my left ankle, although when I said that to Pablo one night, he told me he couldn't see a difference. Maybe it's just me, but I think some sort of war wound remains, the kind that is so subtle only the veterans can tell.

I make an appearance at my last scheduled meeting of the day, which could have been an email. When I leave, I don't have the energy to look at all the messages in my inbox. I glance at the meeting notes I took while on the elevator, disjointed phrases beside dates, tasks that will fill my next few days, my next few weeks. I close my notebook and think that, if I were to die, this diary would present a very boring, unremarkable life. It could belong to anyone. I can't believe that Madrid is glowing with the sweetness of summer and I'm using expressions like "kick off," "status update," "conference call," and "debrief."

I can't remember when I stopped living summer to its fullest and got stuck in one of those stock photos of offices they use in corporate PowerPoints. I glance at myself in the elevator mirror and I don't look as out of place as I'd like to. This woman is nothing special. Pablo wasn't lying: I don't look good; I look sickly. My white dress isn't flattering. My skin is pale from several days of just commuting to and from the office; my eyes are irritated from the halogen lighting and dry because of air-conditioning and computer screens; my body seems to have lost the gleam it used to have before benzodiazepine became one of my main food groups. I'm almost just another office worker. One of the thousands of women I pass in the metro every day whose lives I imagine to be empty and sad. A permanently tired person, always fatigued, insipid, who uses the metro stops of her daily commute as an oasis of escape in which to imagine a better life or lose herself in books about other, better lives. I stopped taking the metro when I couldn't stand to see myself reflected in its treacherous windows, not because of how I looked, covered in a black coat and a gray scarf on cold January mornings, but because it was getting harder for me to distinguish myself from everyone else.

When I leave the elevator, I stop and stare at the rays of sun slipping through the windows. I grab my purse and leave for lunch. I justify it, as if someone cared, by telling myself that because I hadn't had breakfast that morning, I deserve a break a little early. I make a swift exit before any of my coworkers decide to join me.

I'm surprised by an unexpected breeze: the asphalt isn't throbbing with heat and the treetops are swaying slightly. It might even rain today. I walk until I find a half-decent park, which takes longer than predicted because there aren't enough parks in the center of Madrid. I sit in the shade of the Plaza de Oriente, which at this time of day is empty except for two typical middle-aged women feeding the pigeons. I pull out my Tupperware lunch of pasta salad with tuna and hard-boiled egg. I start gobbling down my pasta, like the pigeons side-eyeing me are gobbling down their breadcrumbs.

Pasta, tuna, and hard-boiled egg. The sad, classic lunch of the office worker with no time or imagination makes me think of Rita. I tilt my head back and take pleasure in the sun spilling through the leaves, not even worrying if the ultraviolet rays will someday give me cancer. I don't like thinking about Rita in the office, but I allow myself to occasionally think of her when I leave. I think she would've liked it that way. I pull Rita out of the drawer I stuck her in earlier, put my Tupperware down, and close my eyes. I barely knew anything about Rita's life because at first, all we talked about was Dostoyevsky. Her favorite novel was *The Brothers Karamazov* and, unlike most people, she had actually read it. She loved the line "The more I love humanity in general, the less I love man in particular." She said it made her think about our coworkers.

Rita seemed to have no hope for the people who worked with us; she talked about "out there" and "in here" as if we inhabited two parallel universes with no relationship to each other. She also came up with her own theories about work: for example, Rita had the ironclad conviction that anybody who ended up in HR had to be some sort of psychopath, because they enjoyed firing people, or that those of us in more creative professions had been lonely children with no choice but to use our imaginations to survive. Also about our coworkers, whose lives she invented: "Today Carlos from finance is happy because it's Friday, the only day he has sex with his Catholic girlfriend" or "I'm sure Maika lives in a huge house and has two Dobermans that she can communicate with telepathically."

Talking to Rita during the day helped me to get through the rest of it, and for the first time, I understood why some people liked their jobs. I thought the feeling was mutual, that our friendship was enough to tolerate eight hours every day from Monday to Friday. Having shared interests, like literature, brought us closer, but it was our shared hatred of the place that truly united us. Rita was seething with hatred, but her hatred was justified and she seethed with it in an entertaining way. But even though I knew what she read and what she thought of everyone else, I didn't know what she did with her life outside of work. "Out there."

The only details she revealed about her personal life were about books, and for a while, I didn't question how it was possible to know so little about a person you saw every day. I knew a few things: what neighborhood she lived in (La Latina), because of the bookstores she went to (Sin Tarima, Molar, Traficantes de Sueños); the trips she'd taken recently (Naples, Rouen) to see the settings of the books she'd just read

(Ferrante, Flaubert); that on Sundays she shopped at the book-stalls on Calle Moyano, and that she liked quiet, nearly empty cafés.

Rita wasn't popular at the office—everyone said she was a jerk. Maybe that's why nobody sat with us at lunch. And the truth is, by the standards of the office, she was a jerk. She never did anything beyond the strict definition of her employment contract ("Rita doesn't know how to work with others," "When it's 5:30, she drops her pen," "She's not a team player"), she would yawn in meetings when they went overtime, and once, she told someone in sales that her incompetence wasn't Rita's emergency. I made her a mug with that phrase. She never brought in cupcakes on her birthday, so nobody knew her zodiac sign or how old she was. She also never had drinks after work, or chipped in on gifts for new mothers, and she didn't even bother to make up an excuse for why she wasn't doing it. All she said was "No, thanks, I'm busy" or "I'm not interested."

I imagined she must've had a fascinating life out there, a life none of us were invited to take part in. Not even me. Maybe a book club, interesting friends who wore black turtlenecks and cigarette pants, jazz club evenings, nights at the Teatro Real. Was she like that, or was I idealizing her? Maybe she just left work every day, took a packed metro, and went home to read while she petted her cat, if she had one.

In spite of everything, she was the perfect person to exchange glances with when somebody said something stupid in a meeting. She was also the person who always said "Monday, again," every Monday, as soon as she hung up her coat and sat in front of her computer. And the person you would sometimes catch staring out the window for a long time, mired in her thoughts, with various unfinished tasks opened on her browser, watching the sun fall as the day ran its course.

One day, she didn't show up to work. Nobody was surprised.

Maybe her boss forgot she had taken a personal day, or maybe some emergency came up. The next day, people started asking after her. She had projects due and meetings she hadn't attended. On the third day, HR sent an email informing us of her death. They'd hired a psychologist for those who might need one. We were left in a state of shock that lasted a couple of weeks, just long enough to be respectful of the dead. After that, there were rumors, conjectures, hearsay, more or less kind comments ("How old was she? Wasn't she really young?" "She didn't have any health problems as far as I know." "Was she ill?" "Did she have an accident?" "She got run over by a car." "She fell down some stairs." "She choked on her dinner." "A flowerpot fell on her head while she was taking a walk." "She died of carbon monoxide poisoning." "Was she going through a breakup?" "She asked for some days off to move apartments." "Poor thing." "Was she all alone?" "Did her parents live in Madrid?" "Was she from Madrid?" "Did she have siblings? Cousins? Family?" "Did she have friends?" "Who found her?") and more or less hostile comments ("Did she send you guys an email with the PowerPoint of her last project?" "Who's going to head up the look and feel of the bank project now?" "Fuck, she really left us in the lurch." "Does anyone know the password to her computer?" "Since this Rita thing, I'm up to my eyeballs").

Soon there was a rumor that Rita had died by suicide. Her death seemed too abrupt, and HR was treating the subject with excessive mystery, alluding to "data-protection issues," which suggested her death had been very tragic. No one could confirm it, since no one knew Rita's friends or relatives, but the rumor seemed real. "Lately she seemed more absorbed in her thoughts. I saw it with my own eyes." "She'd been depressed for months. She wasn't in a good place." "She kept it close to her chest, but you could tell." "She'd stopped participating in meetings." "When was the last time you *really* talked to her?"

"You never know what's going on with people." I believed the rumor too. After all, it was a very Russian ending. In my head, Rita, like Anna Karenina, could have thrown herself onto the train tracks. I did the math: the day she died was a Monday.

Rita didn't even get a lousy minute of silence. It seemed the whole office wanted to forget about the incident as soon as possible and act like Rita never existed, especially HR. I guess the thing next weekend will be a way to cover their backs: it's possible Rita's death was in some stupid dossier about employee mental health and well-being.

For months, I'd searched for her whenever someone said something incredibly stupid in meetings, but all I found was my own gaze reflected back at me in the window. I thought of her every Monday as I hung my coat on the same coatrack and sat in the same chair. And I started staring out the window at the Gran Vía, wondering what Rita would think about every time she did it. I never truly got to know her, but I suppose she was thinking about escaping.

A month and a half later, Lorena started working here. The new graphic designer comes into the office every Monday brimming with enthusiasm. Lorena is no Rita, obviously. Lorena is friendly and diligent; she puts in all the hours necessary on each project and never misses drinks after work. Lorena is always in an excellent mood; she drinks matcha tea; she loves *Friends* unironically and still defines herself by her Hogwarts house, despite being thirty-seven. In a horrendous email we received from HR introducing our new colleague, Lorena answered a series of dumb questions about herself so we could "get to know her better," defining herself as a "mother to two fur babies" and attaching a photo of her French bulldogs, saying that her favorite food was "my mother's croquettes" and her favorite phrase was "Sometimes you win, sometimes you learn." My first impulse was to send that email to Rita.

Everybody likes Lorena better than Rita; I know it even

though they can't say it out loud. Everybody except me. Without Rita, I have no one else who gets me. Without Rita, I'm less Marisa, as if a part of me had died with her.

Around the time that Lorena arrived, HR gathered up Rita's belongings and sent an email saying they'd leave them in a meeting room for the day, in case anyone wanted to take a souvenir to remember her by. Afterward, the company would dispose of everything. Like at a wake, an enormous closed cardboard box loomed in the middle of a glass-enclosed room. I kept my eye on it while my coworkers passed by the room, giving it rapid sidelong glances and continuing on their way, not daring to enter. I pretended to work late that day, watching several YouTube videos on climate change and then several YouTube videos explaining how climate change was made up by various governments. Once everyone had gone and the lights dimmed, I went in and grabbed the box. I brought it to my apartment and stuck it in the back of my bedroom closet. The box has been there for eleven months. Rita disappeared a year ago, and I still haven't been able to look inside it.

I open my eyes and observe the plastic container resting on my thighs. I don't feel like eating. I pull out my water bottle and drink it down while I swallow a tranquilizer. I stare at the pigeons for a while longer and feel a stab of tenderness for them. Poor little things, everyone loathes them, they are the most misunderstood species in nature. I like to distance myself from people who believe in a lot of clichés. If they tell me that swimming is the most complete sport, that the best seafood in Spain is in Madrid, that breakfast is the most important meal of the day, or that pigeons are rats with wings, I find it a symptom of intellectual laziness, of not having invested even the slightest thought in questioning whether they actually believe the thing they've repeated millions of times. They think that opposites attract and that, in the end, the extremes always meet. And they're perfectly happy never examining these judgments. In a YouTube documentary about carrier pigeons, I learned how intelligent they are. Among other things, they can recognize their own image in a mirror. Like people, pigeons have self-awareness, and they're even capable of distinguishing humans. They can perfectly identify the adorable old lady who feeds them and the ball-busting little kid who throws rocks at them in the park. I find it fascinating that a pigeon can recognize me while I couldn't distinguish it from a dozen others. I stare at one for a while, wondering if it remembers seeing me at an outdoor table in the Plaza de Olavide and if, later, when I leave, it'll realize and say to itself: "Shit, of course! Marisa!"

I look at my watch. It's 2:30. I gather my things and head back to the office, saying goodbye to my park friends.

"Bye, pigeons!" I say, smiling.

One of the women looks at the other and says, "Poor thing."

The office is now empty. Another advantage of leaving for lunch earlier is you can take much longer than necessary because when you return, no one else is back. It's a quarter to three and I could have stretched it to 3:30. But the pill, even though it calmed me down, also made me sleepy, so I just want to go into my office and try to rest. In fact, if my office didn't have glass walls, it would be the perfect place for a nap.

I look at my emails. More replies from my students, more requests, more tasks, and more "Sorry, I don't know if you got my last email," as if we still can't trust technology. I close my email and open YouTube. I'm recommended an interview from the eighties with director Pedro Almodóvar and artist Fabio McNamara on a program titled *La edad de oro. The Golden Age.* Almodóvar is wearing a white blazer with a black cotton shirt and matching pants. McNamara is made up like a hooker, donning a fantastic blond wig, a bullfighter's jacket, and very tight leather pants. He's blind drunk and smoking on live TV. Every time he makes some inane comment, Almodóvar, who seems more sober than his friend, tries to explain him.

The host, Paloma Chamorro, asks Fabio McNamara which of his professions, which include model, singer, painter, and poet, he prefers. Fabio McNamara responds: "What I like best is being a superficial woman." I guffaw. I wish I could talk about the interview with Pablo. "What is the stupidest thing they've said about you?" asks the host. "Well, that we're boys," responds Fabio. "You give everything to your audience, what do they give you in return?" "They give us cigarettes," says Fabio. In that moment, there are no two people in the world who I like better than Fabio McNamara and Pedro Almodóvar. I wish they were my parents. I'd let them name me Lucifer, teach me to criticize and to sell my body on the streets, just like in their song. The interview ends and they start singing "Satana S.A.," and although I feel slightly empty when they stop speaking, the droning of the song and their shrill voices create a small-town-festival feel that manages to bring me peace.

My office phone rings, and I am forced out of the alternate universe in which my parents are Almodóvar and McNamara.

"Hello?" I reply tersely, hoping the interruption will be as short as possible.

"Marisa?" It's Ramón.

"Hi, Ramón."

"Are you very busy?"

"Kind of, but go ahead," I answer, and I bang randomly on the keyboard.

"Look, I called to tell you something else about the team-building weekend, although I'll have to spoil the surprise for you."

"Oh, no . . ."

"Yeah, sorry, but I think your help is essential. Can you come up and see me for a minute?"

"Sure."

I leave an Excel sheet open on my computer, grab a notepad, and take the elevator to the top floor, where the CEO (a French guy who is hardly ever here) and the department heads have their offices. Ramón is the head of creative and, before working at this company, was the creative director of brands that no longer exist and few people remember. I imagine, from his indeterminate age somewhere between fifty and eighty, that he was in charge of promoting the wheel, horse-drawn carriages, or those bicycles with one enormous wheel in front and a tiny one in the back.

I enter his office, which always smells like tangerine peels. It's large and light-filled, although it looks more like the office of a bank owner than a creative. I think about how we look like our offices, and that if Ramón were a fabric, he'd be a brown polyamide carpet. Ramón has a desk with a ton of papers on it, a sofa with a little side table for coffee, and a couple of armchairs for informal meetings. He points me to an armchair, grabs a stack of papers from his desk, and sits on the sofa. I feel like he's going to psychoanalyze me.

"Would you like a tangerine?" Ramón asks. Every time I visit his office, he offers me one, like a father who worries you're not getting enough fruit.

"No, thanks, I'm good."

"They have a lot of vitamin C."

"That's true, give me one."

Ramón gives me a tangerine and a napkin. I start to peel it because I know it's easier to just eat the tangerine than to refuse it.

"What do you need, Ramón?"

"You see, we're confirming the speakers for the retreat and I wanted to run the selection by you." He hands me four pieces of paper, each with a fact sheet on it. Ramón must be the only person who still prints things out. My hands are sticky from the tangerine, so I tell him to put the pages on the desk. "Oh, yeah, sorry. We'll also have a very special musical performance, but I'll keep that a surprise."

"Thanks," I say, as if he were doing me a huge favor. I eat two pieces of tangerine and wipe my hands. I pick up the pages and begin looking at them.

"The first one is what's now known as a divinity coach," says Ramón. "He was a priest, but he fell in love, with a woman, and left the priesthood." I find it amusing that my boss felt the need to specify that it was with a woman. "He began working at a company and then realized that his religious training was equally valid for corporate culture, and that if a company and its employees practiced Christian values, they'd work together much better."

"Aha," I manage to say, and move on to the next sheet.

"The second one was an Olympic medalist in track and field, but then he lost his legs in an accident." Holy Mother of God. "He gives motivational talks about how to overcome barriers. He's a very good speaker and his story is incredible; my wife recommended him after seeing his video on Facebook, and the truth is he's very interesting."

"OK," I say, moving on to the next page.

"The third one doesn't have legs either."

I eat some tangerine to keep myself from laughing. It's like he googled "legless speakers in Madrid."

"He was an executive at two multinationals, until his accident."

"And he lost his legs?" I ask.

"Exactly. Then he realized what's truly important in life. His talk is more about learning to appreciate the little things, shrug off the everyday stress, and live in the moment."

"Uh-huh."

I move on to the next page, hoping the fourth candidate still has their limbs.

"The last one is a sixty-five-year-old man who, after an entire life devoted to one thing, left it all behind and created a successful food-delivery app." I look at the name of the app, but it doesn't ring a bell. "Now he gives talks about the possibility of changing direction and becoming an entrepreneur at any age because, according to him, age is a question of attitude."

I put the pages down and pick up the tangerine. As always, I don't know why I accepted it, but now I have no choice but to finish. I take another look at the headshots of the four middle-aged men. They all look the same. At least if they were full-body photos, I'd be able to tell who had legs.

"You see, we've almost got everything confirmed, but we have to choose two."

"Yeah . . ."

My boss observes me in silence. This is either the moment when he's expecting my opinion or when he's too afraid to say the thing he wants to say.

"From my perspective, maybe you could eliminate one of the two speakers without legs, it could be . . . it could be a bit repetitive."

"Yes." Ramón hesitates, organizes the papers in front of him. "The thing is that this morning we had a meeting and we realized that, now that the whole equality issue is so in vogue, we don't have any women speakers, and we'd like to have one, so I wanted to ask if you know any women."

"I know a few, to be honest."

He smiles, granting me the slight sass that he would his teenage daughter.

Ever since I joined the company and expressed some vehement opinion in one of those lunches I never go to anymore, I've been branded the office feminist who needs to be consulted on all gender-equity issues. I'm a token; what I read outside of work and the fundamental beliefs I fight for when I'm not too tired are used by the company to improve their image. They always put me on projects that include the word "empowering," and they ask me if certain phrases in our advertisements come off as sexist or could "upset women," as if I knew them all. In the office, men I've never exchanged half a word with ask me absurd things like whether I find reggaeton misogynistic. I'm their own private Mary Wollstonecraft, always available to answer questions that a simple Google search could resolve. Some women in the office, however, try to distance themselves from my feminist image by saying things like "I'm not as radical as Marisa" or "I'm a feminist too, but I love men." Sigh. And here I am now, the only person in the entire office who seems capable of finding a speaker whose ID card says female.

I observe my boss, stifling my desire to smash the tangerine into his face. I can't believe he was able to find two legless men all on his own but needs my help finding a woman.

"What kind?" I ask, trying not to show my irritation.

"I'm not sure," he says pensively. "Maybe a woman who can empower other women, but also men."

"Ah."

I review my mental list of YouTube videos of feminist speeches that I've put on at bedtime, and I consider the ones that seem more decaffeinated, more friendly, more corporate. A part of me is disgusted, like I'm betraying my gender. "Empowering men," as if they need to feel more powerful than they already do. I think about talks on the wage gap, on why women leave their careers to take care of their children, or on the mental burden of housework. I think about talks on destroying gender, sex, the patriarchy. I think about talks on sexism in the workplace, on the need for better applied policies on equality or on companies' lack of real commitment to equity. I know that's not what Ramón is looking for. Instead, he's looking for a speaker of the female gender who can fill an hour with variations on the phrase "Where there's a will, there's a way." Like all the rest, with or without legs. The only thing he's asking me for is a woman. Any woman. He wants to have a speaker who doesn't set off alarms, to cover his back, to save his reputation. Fuck him. I toss out the names of two talks I've seen recently.

"The first one is a menstrual therapist." I see his eyes widen, but he jots down her name. "Don't be frightened, she simply teaches how to understand menstrual cycles to get the most out of them since menstruation is so underexplained; for example, depending on your hormonal cycle, you might be more creative or more self-absorbed or more aggressive, and knowing that could benefit you in your day-to-day."

"And that can be useful to men?"

"Well, I think if they can empathize with a legless man, they can empathize with a woman on her period."

Ramón takes note, but he doesn't seem very convinced.

"The second one is a trans woman who used to be a prostitute and now has her own HBO series. She has a very interesting monologue on YouTube called 'Grab *me* by the pussy,' have a look."

Ramón thanks me. I know he's incapable of telling me he isn't interested in some lady talking about her period or a trans woman who was a prostitute, but he's also incapable of telling me why. If he wants something decaffeinated, friendly, and corporate, he should ask Google. It can't be that hard to search for "coach woman madrid."

I leave his office and go down to my floor, somewhat irritated that work has managed to irritate me so much that the tranquilizing effects of Ativan and Fabio McNamara spouting nonsense have worn off. I check the time: it's four in the afternoon. I've had enough for today. I head home. The day lasted four hundred years. The condensed August air gradually fills my lungs as I walk out onto the street. The bus shelter right in front of the building reads 98 degrees.

V

Passing through the sliding glass doors of the Quevedo Carrefour supermarket is leaving behind a world of chaos and entering a white, aseptic, perfectly organized one where the temperature is correct and you can while away the hours because, like in casinos, the lighting keeps you from knowing the time of day. In a final battle won by capitalism, the Quevedo Carrefour remains open twenty-four hours a day, including most holidays. There isn't a single minute, day or night, when you can't walk in and buy two tangerines, a six-pack of yogurts, a small bag of cashews, and a chocolate bar. The Quevedo Carrefour is like that friend who always picks up on the second ring when you've gotten hammered on a weekday.

On some insomniac nights, my legs bring me automatically to the cheese section, as if my body knows that on the grayest days, my soul needs to observe the perfectly arranged Gouda, Brie, Gruyère, Gorgonzola, and Manchego wrapped profusely in plastic. I feel like a junkie when that happens to me, even though I'm not doing anything illegal. On the back of my neck, I can feel hateful looks from the workers waiting patiently at the register or restocking cereal boxes, enraged that their place of work, uninhabited at four in the morning, only stays open and functioning because of human beings as despicable as me. I feel the guilt in my chest, so I fill an entire basket with products that I won't know what to do with later and, before getting to the checkout, put my cell phone to my ear and pretend to be the supervisor of some hospital emergency room ("Yes, Doctor García speaking") or a surgeon giving orders to a younger doctor ("The carotid shouldn't scare you, José Luis") or a cardiologist just getting out of a complicated operation ("Thanks, we hope the bypass will work"). That way, the workers will stop loathing me and will instead take pity on me and even consider me a superhero with every right to shop while everyone else is sleeping.

That afternoon, I have the Quevedo Carrefour practically to myself. I ignore the prepared food section at the front and head to the fruits and vegetables. Today I need comfort food. I harvest figs and cherries like a rural girl, then avocados and pink tomatoes the size of a newborn's head. I ask for four oysters at the fish counter, grab a can of Santoña anchovies, choose different cheeses and weird marmalades of ginger and bitter orange, pick a bottle of Albariño to wash it all down. I allow some commonplace products to contaminate the gourmet goodies in my basket: toilet paper, napkins, shower gel, hand soap, maxi pads, and tampons. I pay 146.78 euros. I exit Carrefour into the open air, and as I walk home, it seems the two heavy shopping bags are dragging me down to the ground.

When I get home, I put everything away. I serve myself a glass of Albariño and sit down on the sofa to patiently wait for my mother's weekly call. My mother calls me every Tuesday at 6:15. I don't know why or when she chose that day and time, but throughout my entire life, my mother's had an almost military obsession with order and cleanliness. Years later, on YouTube, I came across a series of women and men like her who showed off their immaculate homes and all the products they used. They all had some sort of obsessive-compulsive disorder, so I believed my mother must have that too. Not the incapacitating kind that doesn't let you leave the house for fear of germs or that makes you run back up four flights to make sure you turned off the bathroom light, but the kind that makes her shout at the fishmonger because he's not cleaning the fish the way she likes it, mop a couple of times a day, and feel uncomfortable in restaurants—where she needs to clean her own silverware—and in hotels—where she needs to do white-glove tests. I imagine that's why my mother always calls me at 6:15 on Tuesdays, and also why she never comes to visit. The last time she came was years ago, when I first rented this apartment. After helping me move in, my mother couldn't sleep because the mattress had belonged to a previous tenant, and she spent the weekend cleaning everything from top to bottom. On Saturday, she bought me a new IKEA mattress, and when she left, I had to open the terrace doors because the entire place smelled like ammonia.

At 6:15, my phone starts to vibrate and the screen lights up with a simple *M.*

"Hel . . . , dear."

Another thing is that my mother lives in a small town in a remote part of Guadalajara with very little cell service, and in the winter, she's usually isolated for several weeks because of the snow. Whenever I talk to her, I feel like a contestant on a game show where I have to fill in the blank words to understand the meaning.

"Hello, Mom."

"Can you hear me, we . . . ?"

"More or less."

"Wait. I'll move." I hear my mother shuffling, opening the glass door to the garden and walking on the slate ground. She knows there's a spot, maybe between the rosebush and the almond tree, where she can usually be heard better. "What about now?"

"Yeah, that's better."

"What's new? How are you?"

"Fine, really," I answer quickly, so that no hesitation can make her think otherwise. "How are you both?"

"Well, de . . . Everything's going well here, you know." Silence. I hear some leaves violently ripping, and I can almost see my mother tearing off a branch or weeds she doesn't like the look of. "Your father has taken up ornithology."

"Oh, really? He goes bird-watching?"

I have a sort of mute relationship with my father, which functions in both directions, with the flow of information always passing through my mother. I know about everything he does and everything he's interested in because she tells me, and he knows about everything I do and everything I'm interested in because she tells him. The physical distance between us, and the fact that my father, who's always been a man of few words, is completely inept with technology, don't help the situation.

"Yes . . . at a school . . . near Almiruete . . . of falconry . . ."

"And he likes it?"

"Yes, a lot. Although I'm not convinced it's a good idea to have a falcon in the house, Marisa"—I missed a part here. "They're very rowdy, and all those feathers . . . I don't know if it would be very sanitary."

"Yeah . . . Besides, they have really long talons, Mom, be careful with that." I can almost sense my mother nodding. "They could kill a baby if they wanted to."

"Have you seen Susana?"

I sigh. Susana is my cousin who's been living in Madrid for about ten years now. When we were little, we played together at family gatherings and sometimes after school, but once we became teenagers, we found our own friend groups and lost the connection we shared as little girls. In Madrid, we got together once, nine years ago, for a coffee, while Susana was pregnant with her first child. I think she has three now. Once we'd run out of things to say about our family, we didn't manage to find anything else in common, and neither of us made an effort to get in touch again, although we send each other a WhatsApp every year on Christmas and our birthdays. She usually sends me a photo of her children dressed as Santa Claus. In spite of all that, every week my mother asks me if I've seen her.

"No, Mom, maybe I'll call her this week."

"Good, she's a nice girl, Marisa."

"Sure. Are you doing well?"

"Yes, yes, as always."

There is a silence. It isn't so much uncomfortable as bleak. I realize I'm not sure how to talk to my mother, or what about, and the saddest part is that it's not because we aren't good conversationalists, but because I really don't have anything to say about my life. It fills me with despair to think my mother might pity me and think that, after everything she and my father did to make my life better than theirs (more intense, more interesting, more inspiring), I ended up being a person with a day-to-day life of no consequence. I vaguely recall all those times when she told me she just wanted me to be happy. Happiness, what does that even mean?

Perhaps my mother and I have never had a real conversation: she asked me to be happy, but I never asked her what happiness was exactly and how I could achieve it. My mother and my father always were pragmatic people. If I was cold, they bought me a good jacket. If I wasn't doing well in school, they hired a tutor. If the doctor told them that I was low on calcium or vitamin C, every morning they would give me a glass of milk and an orange juice. They showed love by covering my basic needs: clothing me, feeding me, dressing my wounds every time I fell, and letting me sleep in their bed when I had a nightmare.

"I just want you to be happy" was how my mother encouraged me to move to Madrid and study whatever I wanted at university. She didn't demand I get good grades or find a job right away; she just wanted me to be happy. However, as I started to grow up, our relationship became more complex and, as such, more incomplete. My life was missing a few key adulting pieces. I think of Susana, a good girl, a nursing student, married to a doctor, with an apartment in a wealthy area of Madrid (Arturo Soria, if I'm remembering correctly) and three blond kids who keep them busy and imbue them, in the eyes of our family, with some sort of emotional privilege. It's easier to cover up the uncomfortable silences in family gatherings when there are three screaming kids. Perhaps if I'd been more like Susana, I would have more things to talk about with my mother (like how to get a restless child to sleep, how to handle older-sibling jealousy, how to get bloodstains out of jeans, even how to revive your sex life with a husband who's no longer attracted to you because you've had three babies in five years), but I didn't turn out like her, and my life is as alien to my mother as her expectations for my life are to me.

I don't know when my mother stopped asking me if I had a boyfriend, or if I wanted to have kids, or if I had big plans for the weekend, or where and with whom I was going on vacation. Maybe it was when she discovered I never had a response for any of these questions, or perhaps when she sensed that, in one of those conversations, I might confess something to her, something as horrible as "Mom, I'm not entirely happy."

"Are you eating well?" asks my mother, and I feel her question like one of her homemade ointments on a wound.

"Yes."

"What do you eat?"

"Well, I just did my grocery shopping. I got some cheese, one of those creamy goat cheeses that you like, and some Santoña anchovies."

"How much did they cost you?"

"One hundred and forty-six euros."

"That's outrageous! Madrid, my goodness . . ." She lets out a laugh.

My mother is comforted by the idea that life in the capital is miserable and, as such, rural life is better. She likes to hear me complain about the metro, the crowds, the horrible Christmas lights, and the cost of things.

"Yeah . . . and that's just the anchovies, Mom."

She repeats "That's outrageous" and cracks up laughing. Then she asks, "Are you going to come up . . . soon?"

"I don't know, I have a lot of work right now," I say, feeling a stab of guilt in my chest. "Maybe in September."

"OK, dear." For a moment, my mother seems relieved. "I have to go. I'll call you next week."

"OK, love you."

"I love you, dear. Bye-bye."

I hang up. It's 6:33. I place half an Ativan under my tongue.

I go to the kitchen and busy my brain with the menu for tonight. I position the delicacies onto pretty plates as if I were expecting a visit. I crank up the air-conditioning. I fill another glass of wine, place the oysters on ice, peel a tomato and serve it with olive oil and salt flakes, pull out the anchovies, and prepare a cheese plate with a spoonful of marmalade.

I settle down with my food in front of the coffee table and put on a YouTube video of a Japanese girl eating. I feel in communion with her, sharing supper in silence as if we had that perfect relationship where there's no need to fill it. I pick up an oyster and look to see how many people have watched this video: more than three million. I feel a stab of jealousy, as if I'd just discovered a harmless but worrying infidelity, like a boyfriend flirting with another girl on social media. While she's eating with me, that same girl could be eating dinner with a thousand other people. There are three million other souls whose only company at mealtimes is this woman who devours steaming soups and crunchy vegetables and fish and meat with different sauces, but for some reason I don't feel lonely or sad. I feel happy because I'm not in the office and I'm eating things most people can't afford, in the company of my Eating Beauty. I take generous sips of wine; I eat another oyster, put together an exquisite mouthful of half an anchovy and a piece of tomato; I bite into some cheese on flatbread. The girl in the video exclaims "So yummy!" and I nod. When I've finished, I let the girl finish her dinner in my living room. I don't want to rush her.

I go onto the terrace with my glass of wine and pull an emergency pack of cigarettes out of a drawer. I light one. It's 7:58. I wonder what dreadful meals are being eaten by my neighbors, whom I don't know at all, except for Pablo. I imagine frozen pizzas being shared by second-year medical students who end up arguing because one of them is pro-Franco. I imagine sad grilled chicken fillets with salad from a bag gobbled down in silence by a couple who occasionally comments on the TV news. I think of the journey of a hamburger that someone has ordered and how it will arrive at nine p.m. completely cold and with the bottom of the bun all soggy, and I think about a guy getting his fingers greasy and then leaving an awful review on the app and going to bed with the hope that they'll return his 12.95. If only I could invite all my neighbors over for dinner tonight. I've always thought that, if I married a rich man, I would be a magnificent hostess. My palate has always been a couple of rungs higher up on the class ladder than my pocket.

I stub out the cigarette and go back into the living room. The Japanese girl has finished her dinner and been substituted by a group of Italian women tasting precooked Italian dishes. They are enraged. I gather up the remains of my feast, wash the dishes, open up a plastic container and put some lettuce inside, with the tomato and the leftover anchovies. My sad lunch tomorrow will remind me of the delicacies I dined on tonight. If Proust could remember his childhood by tasting a madeleine dipped in tea, I shouldn't have any problem transporting back to tonight when I eat an anchovy tomorrow. I put the figs in a bowl and sit back down on the sofa, where I watch an hour-long video of a YouTuber reacting to TV shows from the nineties. I can't believe how sweet and fleshy the figs are. I start thinking that I should spend all morning tomorrow getting ahead on my long to-do list, getting it over with so I won't have to think about it anymore. My heart starts racing as I think of everything I'm leaving for some future time. I hate thinking about work outside of work. I decide to take the rest of the Ativan before I go to bed. I eat another fig and listen to the jingle of the game show *What's the Bet?* I think about how the world is filled with repulsive ass-kissers but, on the other hand, from July to September it's also filled with figs.

I don't remember when I fall asleep, but I sleep deeply until the tachycardia returns, banging on my chest at five in the morning. The television is still on, as are the lights and the air-conditioning. I go to the kitchen and open the medicine cabinet: I still have a whole box of Ativan, plus the blister pack in my purse. I try to count how many pills I took last night, but I can't remember. I drink a glass of water and go back to the living room, where I look at the half pill still left on the coffee table. I circle around the table a couple of times, in Shakespearean mode, pondering whether to take or not to take, and finally, I place it beneath my tongue.

I turn off the lights and go back to YouTube. I put on another compilation of children's shows from the nineties, and the opening to *3000 Leagues in Search of Mother* gradually takes me back to my childhood. I watch that, and *Heidi, Girl of the Alps*; *Captain Tsubasa*; *Teenage Mutant Ninja Turtles* . . . At some point between *Recess* and *Pepper Ann,* my brain disconnects.

VI

I wake up two hours later, at seven in the morning, and, against all predictions, feel completely refreshed. It seems like the idea that gave me tachycardia last night had dissolved and transformed me into a productive person who can be part of the system and emerge unscathed. I shower, brush my teeth, put on a shirt and bone-colored linen Bermuda shorts, make some coffee, and start to organize all the things I have to do.

Today it feels like nothing is a big deal: organizing the campaign ideas from the master's students, adding some creative sketches that other people will develop so I can forget all about the Christmas campaign, and searching for examples of creativity workshops so I can plagiarize them for the team-building retreat. No biggie. I remember that playing office worker is easy if you know how. I decide to put a carrot in front of my face. If I take my vacation time right after the retreat, I'll avoid the official return to work after the summer. I think about islands. I want to bathe in lovely coves, day drink, and go to sleep at 9:30 every night. I don't know where I'll go, but I won't be here.

I drink another coffee while I scroll through Twitter. Another powerful man has been accused of sexual misconduct by ten women and, to no one's surprise, a bunch of men are questioning their testimony, because maybe those women were after the powerful man's money. The internet is exhausting, especially if you're a woman. I retweet a couple of feminist accounts because, luckily, on the internet you can always find someone who's said what you're thinking not only before you, but better than you, so you don't even have to make the effort to articulate your own thoughts. I look at an account called Kids Doing Stupid Stuff. There's a video of a boy getting hit by a giant plastic ball, one bounce and he falls into the pool. I'm cracking up. I give it a like but decide not to retweet it because my previous retweet was too serious and I don't want anyone thinking I lack social cues. I finish getting ready and head out onto the street.

To avoid the ceremonial morning slump and my fantasies of getting run over, I decide to listen to something upbeat. I put on my headphones and sunglasses and listen to "Work It," by Marie Davidson. "You wanna know how I get away with everything? I work. All the fucking time." I feel that today I can adopt that personality. Be the shark, the winner; take on the personality of women who've turned work into some sort of sacred virtue, the way motherhood used to be, and who hang up photos in their offices with the hashtag #GirlBoss. I'll turn into capitalism's idea of a feminist for the next eight hours. An überwoman who can handle everything. The kind who has routines from five to nine and then from nine to five. Some sort of cyborg promoted by business schools, with all the positive qualities associated with women but without any of the bad ones: the disciples of Sheryl Sandberg who want to break the glass ceiling with their stiletto heels and leave the broken glass on the floor for the South American cleaning lady to deal with, and whose idea of equality is having a parking spot in the fancy area reserved for the executive board. I enter the office feeling confident. It can't be a coincidence that I'm wearing a shorts suit today.

On my way to my office, I see Natalia looking at me with eyes like saucers.

"Thank God you're here, Marisa," she says in agitation. "We have an enormous problem, a threat to our reputation, we have to talk to Ramón."

I look up at the halogen ceiling lights and sigh. All this has to happen on the one day I was planning on getting some work done. I recoup the feelings I had on my walk here. Work it. Everything's fine.

"Do I have time for a coffee?" I ask, entering my office with Natalia tagging along like a hungry little poodle.

"I don't think so, this is an extreme situation, we have an incredibly angry client and . . ."

"OK, don't worry, let's go see Ramón."

We ascend the elevator in silence. I can almost hear Natalia's heart beating. The problem with overidentifying with your job is that you become affected by these kinds of situations. You say things like "We won an account" but also "We lost an account." Losing a client feels like a personal failure, as if you were dumped for a new lover or like your kid prefers his dad's new girlfriend. Natalia nervously taps her notebook against her chest, and I notice her perfect French manicure. I realize that I desperately need for her not to destroy that manicure with her nervousness.

"I've never been on this floor," says Natalia when the elevator opens.

"Then, welcome."

I lead Natalia to Ramón's office. I'm flooded with the smell of tangerines as soon as we enter. Natalia looks around like a kid at an amusement park. Ramón is with Maika, who mutters a clearly audible "About time" when we walk in, as if she were trying to make Natalia more tense than she already is. I detest her with every fiber of my being. I detest her suit jacket, her luxury-brand purse, her aura of always wanting to speak to the manager. I detest her high-school-bully attitude, her way of exerting subtle but constant pressure on her coworkers, the ease with which she asks you to do things that aren't part of your job and how, when she manages to get you to do them, acts like she was the one doing you a favor and, as such, you owe her something. I detest her loyalty to the company, her possession of it, her conviction that work makes us better people. I detest her smug expression when she closes a deal, when a project comes off, when she gets her way. And I hate when something doesn't succeed and her carrion-eater gaze starts looking for people to blame. For a second, I think she can sense the hatred she provokes in me and she brazenly holds my gaze. I'm the one who ends up lowering her eyes. I'm terrified that witch can read my thoughts.

Ramón points to the sofa. "Sit down, ladies. This could take a while—would you like a tangerine?"

"No, thanks," I respond.

Natalia remains silent.

"OK, fine, let's get to the point: our reputation is on the line. Maika has filled me in on what happened, but I'd like for us to review it together and find the most appropriate solution. The client is very angry and we can't afford to lose an annual account of that size."

I'm incapable of remembering the number of times I've heard the phrase "Our reputation is on the line." Those words strike terror and respect, almost as if we were dealing with the National Intelligence Center, when really we're talking about people complaining about a tweet. Endangered reputations are nothing more than screwups, a series of mistakes bound together by negligence and ignorance that in the era of social media blow up in the faces of clients who've never had to face criticism before.

"It's 420,000 euros a year, ladies, this is no joke," points out Maika haughtily.

Client: An appliance brand; my company runs their social media accounts, among other things. Facts: Yesterday, at around eleven p.m., coinciding with the broadcast of a cooking show, the Twitter account of this appliance brand decided to join in on the trending topic of the moment (#TopKitchen7) by tweeting: "Be honest, who's a better cook? RT your wife FAV your mother #TopKitchen7." The account, which barely has 6,700 followers (because what kind of mentally ill person wants constant updates on new washing machines?) was quite controversial among those following the hashtag. The tweet was immediately erased, explains Maika, but there were screenshots taken and shared by a couple of people with a big following. Feeling morally superior to a dishwasher, a lot of people commented on how sexist and inappropriate the tweet was and suggested boycotting the brand. Some media outlets that are only read by the journalists who work for them gathered the testimony of the tweeters and wrote articles on how the brand was "setting the social networks aflame" and that they'd gotten "serious blowback" online. Since then, Maika has responded with a total of seventeen calls to the client and informed the brand that she was about to enter into a special crisis cabinet to find the best solution.

The crisis cabinet is me, Ramón, and Natalia.

"I'm thinking of sending out a tweet saying that we're going to fire the community manager and distance ourselves from the message," says Maika.

"No," I reply.

"Why not?"

"Because then the brand will look like a jerk who kicked a poor young guy to the curb over a tweet."

More facts: My company signs an advertising contract with the appliance brand for a total of 420,000 euros a year. My company decides to take a total of 4,800 euros out of that 420,000 to pay a freelancer 400 euros a month before taxes to manage the brand's Facebook, Twitter, and Instagram accounts. They promise that freelancer that the work will only take an hour a day, and that our company will take care of managing the client, the monthly posting calendar, and the social media assets. The freelancer only has to suggest ideas for the monthly calendar and give personality and voice to the posts. "Make it look like it's not a refrigerator talking, you know?"—whatever that means. The hour a day turns into many more hours because the brand has a lot of "buts," and what seems like 400 euros of easy money becomes daily torture. There are always changes, there's always a "give it another try," there are always three or four nos before a yes. The latest feedback the freelancer received from my company was that the brand wants to be "more a part of the cultural conversation" using "hashtags and threads" in a "fun and relatable" way. The freelancer offers up a series of ideas, my company offers up others, and the client offers up some more. Some are approved; others are rejected. Among those approved was the idea of live-tweeting the most viewed cooking show on TV. The tweets have to be fun and relatable, clever and amusing. The brand as friend. The community manager, who is a twenty-four-year-old guy tweeting from his house, doesn't decide what's posted or when; he's following the instructions of a brand he only has contact with through the broken telephone that is my company. Mistakes bound together by negligence, ignorance, and companies who want to get the greatest profit out of 420,000 euros. Someone must have suggested writing that tweet, and someone in my company must have approved it. It's clever and fresh! It's funny because it's true! It's part of the conversation! It's just what the client's looking for! Nobody saw anything wrong with asking whether mothers or wives are the better cooks. Or maybe the twenty-four-year-old guy saw something wrong, but he didn't have the energy to fight over posting or not posting a tweet for an appliance company that was making him spend his Tuesday night watching a piece-of-shit TV show, instead of having sex with his girlfriend, for 400 fucking euros a month, which, come to think of it, is practically the entire amount he pays in taxes. And that was how the tragedy happened.

"Well, what do you suggest then?" asks Maika scathingly.

"I think the best thing would be to send out an apology," answers Natalia. "Something like 'We regret the unfortunate tweet from last night and we thank everyone who made us aware of the terrible mistake we made.'"

"Yes, sure," says Maika, "and we can give them a blow job while we're at it."

"It's a matter of choosing the right words," I intervene, "but Natalia is right, we have to apologize."

"OK, well, I'm going to call the brand," announces Maika, standing up, visibly nervous: shark in the company, little fish with the client. "Or maybe you should write the message for me first?" She is stammering. "Yes, it's better to offer them something as soon as possible, and I think you should be at the meeting." She turns on her heels about to leave Ramón's office. "I want the message in twenty minutes, and we'll talk to the client in twenty-five."

I must admit I've always wanted to leave a meeting like that. Natalia looks at me; Ramón looks at me. I am going to have to write the message. I stand up and wander around the office in silence. There are several rules for apologies online. The first is that you must accept your mistake. Don't try to avoid it or blame someone else. For example, the intern. The second rule is that you must never ever apologize to "those who might have been offended" or you will make it much worse. It was your tweet that was offensive, not people's reactions. I can't remember any rules beyond that because I learned them from the Twitter thread of a "digital marketing expert" who was so boring and cringey that I blocked him. Now I kinda wish I still followed him.

"The best thing is to be clear and honest." I look at Natalia. "Take notes, please. Something like: 'Last night we made a mistake and we want to apologize. Our company supports equality between men and women, and we realize that yesterday's tweet was sexist.'"

"Isn't 'sexist' an awfully strong word?" asks Ramón.

"We're not saying we're sexist, just that our tweet was sexist," I clarify. "Do we have any statistics on equality for the brand?"

"Not too long ago, we did a campaign for them about their breast cancer donations."

"Well, we have to stick that in somewhere." God, I really disgust myself. "Something like . . . 'We've been working for years to make women's lives better' or 'Our organization such-and-such donates X amount of money to so-and-so.'"

"Great," says Natalia, her pen practically setting her notebook aflame.

We revise. We add nuance. We tweak the language so the brand stops being public enemy number one. What's weird is that no one will remember this tomorrow because everyone will be too busy hating on some woman who said her son eats chickpeas instead of Bollycaos. We finish the official message, and Natalia and I take the elevator down to Maika's floor. Natalia seems calmer on this second trip.

"You think it'll be fine?" she asks me.

"Honestly, I don't know," I reply sincerely. Although not with enough sincerity to add "and the truth is I don't care."

Maika is in her office. She already has the client on the other line. She waves us in through the glass door.

"Diego, the creatives are here."

"So you're the ones who screwed up?" we hear from the phone.

I imagine the typical asshole with a department store suit enjoying the moment when he can finally humiliate a couple of strangers as a way to forget all the times he'd been humiliated at work.

"Well, do you have a solution yet, or are you planning on waiting another twelve hours?"

"We've got it," I say, ignoring his impertinence, and I read the message to him. "'Last night we made a mistake and we want to apologize. Our company firmly supports equality between men and women, and our tweet, with its attempted humorous tone that we now realize was unfortunate and sexist, is not in line with the values we've held for more than fifty years, as evidenced by our constant commitment to the fight against breast cancer. We thank everyone who drew our attention to this mistake.'"

Absolute silence. Maika is staring intensely at the telephone. Natalia looks at me. I look at Natalia.

"Sounds correct," says Diego. "You could add somewhere that our staff is fifty-five percent women."

"Of course," replies Maika quickly. "Whatever you say."

"Well, I would say this should never happen again, we can't screw up like this, and I promise you that, as far as we're concerned, we're going to fire everyone who approved that shitty tweet, and I hope you do the same. Good day to you all."

End of the call. Maika looks at us without seeing us, her eyes open very wide and a smile frozen on her face. If she were a cartoon, dollar signs would appear in her pupils.

"OK, very well, ladies, get to work!" she exclaims finally, slapping the table.

Not even a sad little thank-you.

Natalia and I leave Maika's office and go to our floor. There we send the apology message to our design team. Once tweeted, it doesn't get as much attention as the offensive tweet, as expected, but the brand is more or less content. They see it as an opportunity to mention their female-staff stats and the breast cancer stuff. As a result, a ton of accounts with little Spanish flags beside their names start insulting the feminists who criticized the original tweet. "You don't care about women with cancer, bitch?" writes someone called Astray88. And that is Twitter's life cycle. Now all the fascists will buy our client's washing machines. And those of us who work in their brand communication, who've become so useless we don't even know how to post an apology on social media, will keep getting paid for a job that a well-trained monkey could do. And they all live happily ever after.

I sit in my office for three hours after the tragedy. I no longer have the desire or energy to do everything I'd planned on doing. Starting the morning by talking to four people put me off-kilter. I consider taking half a pill for my anxiety, but that would make me sleepy. I go into the kitchen to make a coffee and drink some water. Natalia has hidden her capsules and hung up signs saying we're being recorded, so I have to steal them from somebody else. I need tachycardia to give me some sense of impending danger in order to focus on my work. I use two capsules to make a double. I go back to my office and look through my email. I have a congratulatory message from Ramón about how we resolved the situation this morning, and I forward it to Natalia so she'll be happy. In the email, he refers to her as Vanesa. Some master's students have sent me their ideas. I download one of their PowerPoints, but as soon as I open it, I feel like life is meaningless. I decide to think I've already done something important today and deserve a break.

I put on a video of a little dog who gets super happy when

his owner returns from Iraq. I feel like crying. I think about that poor little dog, about whether he knows that his owner is coming back from having killed a ton of people. Will the dog smell the stench of war? Will he notice any substantial change in his owner? Something primal, intense, radical: the scent of death. It's too sad to think that the dog could smell a change in his owner and not recognize him. Maybe someone should make a movie about that from the dog's point of view. I jump when Natalia knocks on the door, which I completely forgot to close, and I stop the video that YouTube recommends of another dog greeting his owner who's returning from another war.

"Come in," I say, straightening my back.

"What a morning," she says, smiling. And I sense that Natalia, in a way, enjoyed this morning and all the adrenaline it generated. I can tell that she felt useful, and she loved it.

It terrifies me that she thinks that way. That work has become her source of recognition and that, like someone in a casino, she is getting addicted to the compensations, which, in this case, come in the form of congratulatory emails where her boss refers to her by someone else's name.

"Crazy," I respond, shaking my head.

"Are you very busy now?"

I open up the worthless Excel sheet.

"Yeah, but go ahead."

"I already have the insights you asked for in a presentation. There are some pretty interesting market studies about the evolution of Christmas shopping that might be useful to you when developing creative approaches."

"Send it to me and I'll have a look. I've got some thoughts and I'll see if we're aligned."

"Great." Natalia stands there with the half smile of a dimwit, and I understand what she wants is a pat on the back.

This is how it all starts. This is the exact moment when she starts to sell her soul. I don't feel like her boss, I don't feel like a boss at all, I give no importance to what I do and sometimes I forget how valuable it is for other people.

"By the way, Natalia, congratulations, you did good today."

Her face lights up with a smile that reveals all her teeth.

"Thank you so much, Marisa. I learned a lot."

She leaves my office and I feel tenderness toward her. If we were in a bar instead of the office, and I'd had three glasses of wine, I would tell her that when you ask for a compliment, you usually get a compulsory one. I would tell her that it's like saying "I love you" and expecting an I-love-you in return and, when you don't get it, feeling worthless. Before she sits down at her desk, I already have her email in my inbox. She must have written the draft before she came over. She's attached a Power-Point with twenty-seven slides analyzing Christmas shopping habits that I don't feel like reading right now, so I gather up my things and tell Natalia I have a client lunch.

I don't need to check Google; I know exactly what I want: a charming Japanese restaurant attended by the top brass and people who want to seem important, where the staff is very friendly and the food is exquisite. It's a fifteen-minute walk, and when I'm at the door, I realize I'm salivating like a dog in front of a steak. The restaurant's dim lighting makes you never sure what time of day it is. It's one of those places where you're offered fine spirits after your meal, so you linger, allowing deals to close and legs to open. They seat me at a small table and I order the prix fixe menu. I look around while I wait for the first course. I'm surrounded by the sort of people I detest most in this world: somewhat important men in suits. Men who sit with their legs spread wide and order without looking at the waiters, as if they're an interruption. Men with overwhelming confidence who think that their every word deserves to be listened to and applauded.

"What I say is that for me it's clear: step up or step aside," says one of them to another, who is identical to him.

They bring me a wakame-and-cucumber salad. There is only one other woman in the restaurant, but she makes me feel like I'm of a different species. Silky dark hair with a precise cut that hangs below her shoulder blades, black tube dress, and high heels. She has her back to me, but judging by the man ogling her, I assume she has nice tits. She laughs, throwing her head back, subtly running the tip of her shoe along the man's leg, gently touching his hand so he thinks he's saying something truly interesting. She knows how to be seductive. I feel over-whelmed by all that femininity, as if it had been distributed irregularly among us. For some of us, being a woman is easy, while for others, it's like putting on a dress two sizes too big. As I chew my wakame salad, I'm incapable of discerning whether she's his wife, his lover, or a prostitute. Although women like her aren't prostitutes; they're escorts.

"This life is for winners, Josemi," says the man at the next table. "On the battlefield, you can't stop to think, you have to see the fear you provoke in others' eyes and act; you don't want to be the guy with fear in his eyes."

When I finish my wakame salad, they bring me some assorted sashimi, which I eat while I listen, spellbound, to the men's conversation. I don't know where they get all that rage, that competitiveness, that way of seeing and dividing the world into winners and losers. I find it strange how some men use war and sports terminology when they've never been in a war and haven't kicked a ball since high school. Preparing for battle, winning the war, destroying the enemy. How can they see themselves as soldiers and warriors when they're inside apartments filled with gray IKEA furniture with greasy paper bags from Just Eat piling up in their dirty kitchens? How are they capable of dissociating between the little men they are and the great men they were promised they would become? I think about whether they're loved by someone, who that could be, and in what way. Who would be the woman—because they're always women—to make herself smaller so that a man can continue seeing himself as big? Big like Alexander the Great, like Julius Caesar, like Christopher Columbus. Big like all those glorious epics they've been imbibing since their earliest infancy. I think about how those men are capable of fooling themselves, but, most of all, how they manage to get the world to sustain that deception. I think about whether at night, right before going to sleep, they feel like impostors or if they've swallowed their own lie and sleep like babies. No one talks back to them, no one contradicts them, no one tells them to shut up. No one says that "step up or step aside" is a total crock of shit. And so, it's almost normal that those men think of themselves as warriors, because by molding the world to their delusions of grandeur, they've already won their own battle. I'm about to interrupt them. To do something as cinematic as to say "I couldn't help but overhear your conversation, and I'm very interested in knowing what you guys do: Are you gladiators? Corsairs? Are you perhaps conquistadors?" But then the waitress takes away my empty plate and brings me the main course: okonomiyaki.

I've never been to Japan, I don't know if this okonomiyaki has anything to do with the original recipe or if it's the equivalent of ordering a paella in Times Square; the only thing I know is that the flavors and the preparation make me forget who I am and how I feel during the time it takes me to devour it.

"Marisa?"

I look up from my plate. It's the other woman in the restaurant. The only other one. The wife slash lover slash escort. I stare at her without understanding how her cherry-colored lips spoke my name. She smiles at me, I smile at her, and I do some mental archaeology, trying to place this woman in some meeting at my company, maybe an executive from a cosmetics company. I got nothing.

"Marisa! It's Elena, from college."

I short-circuit because I remember Elena perfectly, my friend Elena, but I can't recognize her in the woman standing before me. Elena, the girl I went to museums with, smoked joints and tried to watch Bergman films but ended up watching American teen movies with. Elena, always dark, skinny, with an aura of mystery around her, like a vampire waking as night falls and allowing the shadows to muffle yesterday's hangover. Elena, who stuffed her face with junk food every time we got high and then forgot to eat anything the rest of the day. Elena, with whom I would laugh until both our stomachs hurt and with whom I would talk about the future, always as an infinite possibility, always imagined in a completely different way than it would end up being. She was my friend, my best friend, until we found boyfriends and started working and saw each other less and less and finally lost that intimate connection that can only be shared by single people with a lot of time on their hands.

"No way," I say, and I stand up to hug her.

"Honey, wait for me outside," she tells her companion while she hugs me. We observe each other with curiosity and wariness. "I know, I've changed a lot. I have boobs now."

"Elena . . ." I murmur, looking at her. "I didn't recognize you."

Elena's presence finally made the men at the next table shut up for a couple of minutes. If only I could shrink her and carry her in my bag so I could pull her out and put her on the table during meetings with multinational executives. Elena is unreal, like someone on a magazine cover, designed in a laboratory for teenagers to jerk off to. Tits, ass, flat stomach, and a straight white smile. I can't stop looking at her.

"I know, I know, don't mention it. What are you up to?" she asks. "What's going on in your life? What are you doing here?"

"Eating okonomiyaki," I reply.

"It's the best!"

"And what about you? What's going on with you?"

"A lot of things," she answers, smiling and taking me by both hands. "I'm so happy to see you."

"Me too," I reply with the same smile.

"Why don't we get together and catch up? I don't know, is that a stupid thing to say? That we get together? You probably don't want to, don't feel obligated."

"No, no," I say hastily. I don't know why we are so nervous. "That would be great."

"OK, but really? When? Tonight?"

"Today?"

"Are you busy?"

"No, not really," I reply. "I never have much to do."

"Great, me either. Let's get together later, I'll give you my number."

She types it into my phone, hugs me again like a Sicilian mother, and walks out, leaving behind a trail of expensive perfume. I take the first bite of my okonomiyaki while I think about Elena. I wonder if she saw me as transformed as I saw her, and I consider how I didn't lie once during our entire conversation. It's true that I felt joy when I recognized her, and it's true that I never have much to do.

"Did you see that?" says the guy at the next table. "What a sexpot. If I had a woman like that, I'd never leave the house." They laugh like orangutans.

"Shhhhhh," I hiss without looking at them. It's no longer just that their existence annoys me; it's that their voices aren't letting me think.

They fall silent and, before long, continue discussing the battles they have to win, but they've lowered the volume a few decibels.

I'm feeling somewhat dizzy at the thought of Elena and me getting together later today. I'm afraid that the joy I'm feeling now will disappear. Or that reality will bury it deep. I don't know if we can act like we used to because we're not the girls we used to be. And I don't know if the women we are now will connect. I finish eating and pay the check. Before I get up from the table, I take half a pill for anxiety.

I leave the restaurant thinking about all those people that I've lost track of. Some of them weren't important: we simply were forced to share four walls and a ceiling for a few years. At primary school, in high school, university, my first job. But some of them were important to me. It's as if they left a small mark on my skin that makes me smile whenever I catch a glimpse of it. I have preemptive nostalgia thinking that one day I could lose Pablo just like I lost other people. I feel the same way now about Elena. Losing her the first time wasn't hard; it was almost natural, a decision made by the capricious gods of life's twists and turns, to whom we mortals are mere puppets. But if I get her back and lose her again, I'd probably feel a bit sad.

The heat in Madrid is suffocating and I decide to walk in the shade. I've never had a group of girlfriends. I've always been a satellite person, part of many groups but never the glue that held them together. I've worked better alone, or in small groups, except for when I'm high and can interact with a lot of people at once and for several hours. Elena was different. When I was by her side, it was clear who was the star, but she allowed me to be the tail of her comet. Elena talked a blue streak, had strong opinions and the power to make a room fall silent once she opened her mouth. And yet she was also a good listener. She had the ability to look at you and make you feel seen not only by her, but by everyone. Like today. Just by saying my name, she made me remember who I used to be, as if that Marisa only existed in the presence of that Elena.

VII

Elena tells me to meet her at 7:30 at a corner bar in the Plaza de las Comendadoras.

I get out of the shower and lay two outfits on the bed. The first one is a crop top and matching shorts with colorful geometric shapes. The second one is a red cotton blouse and lightweight jeans. I haven't worn either in centuries. I pace around the room, edgy, forgetting where things are (my deodorant, my sandals, some hoop earrings). I feel the way I did at twenty years old before a first date, afraid I won't make a good impression, afraid that Elena will think I'm just a boring person who works in a boring company and has a boring life. I dry my hair upside down, put on the hoops I've finally found, powder my face with bronzer, and paint on thick black eyeliner. I try on both outfits and parade in front of the mirror, pretending that I'm a stranger I'm seeing for the first time to figure out what impression I'd make. I opt for the colorful matching set because it makes more of an impact. I put on some black heeled sandals and grab a tiny green purse with fringe that reaches my knees. I check the time and it's only 6:45.

I sit on the edge of my bed and go on Instagram. I find Instagram the most vacuous of all the social networks. It's like a boutique window for beautiful things and ugly babies. It should be illegal to photograph children under two. You should get a letter from Silicon Valley saying your account's been suspended and you have to pay a $500 fine. There's no such thing as an attractive baby, no matter how you look at it. They are like compressed old people. Supposedly human beings, the world's most intelligent animal, must be born earlier than the rest because our brains are so big our heads would kill our mothers if we came out fully developed. Nobody finds it odd that babies come out half-baked and with Play-Doh heads. Picking up a baby is like picking up a porcelain vase. I think about this as I scroll past a photo of a baby inside a blow-up pool, but I like a cat photo by the same woman, making my principles clear to the algorithm.

I decide to look at the profiles of people I went to university with. Elena doesn't have Instagram. Or at least she's never followed me and I've never found her. One classmate whose hair I held back so she could puke at a rager now lives in London and posts photos of old Victorian doors and avocado toasts accompanied by flat whites. Another classmate, whom I hooked up with during sophomore year, returned to his hometown, Valencia, and has a shop for secondhand designer furniture, a husband who looks like his twin brother, and a baby they bought in Ukraine. Another became a tattoo artist. Another does the PR for a music festival. All I know about them through these anodyne, happy photos is what they do or where they live. I don't know if their lives are disappointing or if they are content. I don't know if they take pills to fall asleep or if they sleep deeply every night. I don't know if the woman who works in music has fucked some member of a popular band or had to travel to another city to buy a shitload of drugs for some DJ. I don't know if any of them have been sick recently. I don't know if they're suffering, if they've had a psychotic break, if they hate the place they live in or the job they have. I don't know if they're idiots or highly intelligent. If they vote right or left. If they call their mothers once a week or never. I don't even know if their mothers are alive or dead. "Who are you?" I'd like to ask the void of my feed. "Do you have any food allergies?"

I go to my profile and look through my photos. The last three are an image that Pablo took early this summer of my back on my terrace with the caption "First cockroach spotted in the city," a photo of a French bulldog with the caption "Dogs are my favorite people," and that meme of a dog sitting in a kitchen engulfed in flames that says, "This is fine." I start giggling at the thought of my own online image. I don't know that person either. I don't even remember whose bulldog that was. Despite my total rejection of places like Instagram, there are days when I feel I need to inhabit it. It's like I need to remind everyone else, and myself, that I'm here too. I look at the time and it's five after. I take a shot of vodka, rinse my mouth with Listerine, and head outside.

When I get to the bar, Elena is already sitting at a table. She's changed her clothes too: she's wearing a cool bone-colored linen dress, with large tortoiseshell buttons and flat sandals. She's pulled her hair back and now looks like a sexy Italian actress from the sixties. I go to the table, and we greet each other effusively again, in an embrace that seems to last as long as the time we've gone since seeing each other, and I sit down beside her.

"I ordered a glass of wine, but if you want, we can order a bottle for the two of us," she says.

"Sounds good."

The waiter uncorks a bottle for us. I serve myself and take a long eager swig. The people next to us order rounds and laugh. Some others are like vultures, pacing around trying to find a free table. Children are making a racket in the park; balls are flying, old ladies repeating "Be careful!" and asking the air

"Whose child is this?" But children in parks don't belong to anyone. It's their kingdom and that should be respected.

"You look so pretty," says Elena.

"What? I'm . . ." I glance at my outfit and realize I probably should have ironed it before leaving. "I'm in disguise."

"No, you were in disguise this morning."

I look at her, thinking that she's right.

"You're the one who's stunning, Elena. I almost didn't recognize you."

"I had work done."

"On what?"

"Well . . . everything." She looks down at herself and waves her arms like a hostess displaying a product on a shopping channel. "Practically everything. I'm filled with plastic, I'm like the Atlantic Ocean."

"But you're happy." I don't ask; I declare.

"Well." She takes a sip of her wine. "Sometimes, like everybody. Right now, yes."

And it's that simple, as simple as not replying "Fine" when someone asks you "How's it going?" Elena starts to tell me the story of her life since we grew apart, all in detail, with some branches that emerge and bear delicious and unexpected fruits, while others dry up and go nowhere. Sometimes she returns to forgotten moments in the story after getting distracted, like the best stories, the ones that have no beginning and no end.

She tells me that her little brother went to med school, that she found out that her stomach hurt because of lactose intolerance and she really misses cheese. She tells me a funny story about the flight back from a trip to Brazil, where she sat next to a guy who'd won a reality show in the nineties and acted like he was a Hollywood star even though nobody knew who he was. She tells me that she thought about me a lot when she finally read a beloved book I'd given her. She tells me she thought about calling me. She tells me that she doesn't have a lot of friends. And she asks, asks, asks me stuff. I tell her about my breakup with the boyfriend she knew. I tell her about a gaslighting episode when he tried to convince me that they stopped selling Parmesan cheese in Spain because he couldn't find it in the supermarket. I tell her how when I was at a beach on Naxos, in the Aegean Sea, everything was so lovely that I burst into tears while swimming. I tell her that my job is hell. I ask about her life. I ask what she does for a living. I tell her that, even though I hadn't recognized her in the restaurant, now she seems like the same person I used to know, because I'd gotten used to her new face.

"Umm, you remember Gustavo? My college boyfriend?"

"The one with really short legs?"

"No, that was Pedro, we used to call him Stumpy Pedro, remember?" she says. "Pedro was the last one you knew? You didn't meet my right-wing boyfriend?"

"Doesn't ring a bell, I think we weren't as close by then."

"That's true." She sighs. "Well, let's see, Gustavo and I started dating senior year, he was studying business administration and he was really loaded. As soon as he graduated, he set up a restaurant—that was his thing, restaurants. Now he has three more throughout Madrid."

"Aha." I take another sip of wine. "What kind of restaurant?"

"Mmmmm . . . well, it was one of those typical restaurants that are popular now, with big wooden tables where they make you sit with strangers, velvet pastel chairs, and a lot of indoor plants. It's that kind of restaurant where the cocktails are at least 12 euros and the classic tapas have a touch of fusion that they define as 'Madrileño chic.' And they all have women's names: Casa Manolita, Villa Paquita, Doña Ciruela."

" 'Ciruela' isn't a woman's name," I say, laughing.

"It should be," she says, and lifts her glass in a toast. "But anyway, who cares what kind of restaurant it is?"

"It helps me to know what kind of a person he was."

"He was a neoliberal who opened up a restaurant for neoliberals." She polishes off her wine and serves herself another glass. She refills mine without asking, spilling some on the table. "I must admit I was fascinated; he bored me incredibly, but I was very interested in his world, with all those friends who were the sons of politicians and bankers, you know? People completely ignorant of all the privileges they'd had since birth, just ignorant period, because they were really dumb, they hadn't read a single book in their lives besides the fucking biography of Steve Jobs or some shit like *Who Moved My Cheese?*"

"Yeah." I nod. "The kind that are super blond as kids, but when they grow up all start to look like José María Aznar."

"Exactly! You read my thoughts. And who suddenly get really into something and won't stop talking about big data or cryptocurrencies and they invest all their savings into shit like that."

"And then they kill themselves."

Elena lets out a really loud laugh, throwing her head back.

"So, what happened with Gustavo? Are you married to him?"

"No way, man, I'm not married to anybody," she answers, laughing. "I was still into my artsy-fartsy stuff. I worked an easy job at a small art gallery and then at home I made collages."

"And then?" I asked, truly interested, truly wasted.

"I realized that I was just the woman Gustavo wanted: a pretty, charismatic, artistic, left-leaning girlfriend to add a touch of punk to his life so he'd stand out from the rest of his fascist friends who were going to marry brunettes who wear brown boots." She takes another sip of wine and looks at me keenly. "I realized my life was a performance: I didn't love him, I didn't particularly like that life, and I wasn't entirely myself when I was with him. It was all an act." Then she grows silent and observes me carefully, as she used to do in university when she wanted to see if I was also feeling the joint we just smoked.

I drink more wine and look back at her. I observe how

her cheekbones are more prominent than when she was the same weight as a sparrow, how her once thin lips now stick out voluptuously. She lets me stare because she's convinced I understand her. And I think I understand her just like I did when we were twenty-one, when we would sit in a doorway not far from here with mixed drinks and cigarettes and talk about artists, some living but mostly dead. I now observe the curve of her plastic breasts. I process the information she's just revealed to me, which she's probably never revealed in that same way to anyone else, and I find her the most interesting woman on the planet.

"And you kept it up," I reply.

Elena looks at me with very wide eyes and nods. Why stop there? she asked herself. Why not explore other paths of normative femininity? Why not exploit them? Why settle for being the arty wife of the owner of three restaurants when you could be something more? Why not take full advantage of a nice face and body? Why not accept once and for all that there are men who are always going to look down on us and who deserve to be stripped of their money? Rich men, important men. She tells me: "The paths of femininity are inscrutable." And she also tells me: "The heteropatriarchy is always going to see us as objects." And then she says it in another way because she's so drunk she's unaware she's already arrived at the crux of the matter. She also confesses that sometimes she looks in the mirror and likes what she sees and other times she looks and doesn't know who she is, and I tell her that I understand.

Elena convinced Gustavo to pay for a breast augmentation, and Gustavo, pleased as punch, paid for it. Then Elena started receiving more attention from the male clientele at the art gallery, and she thought that a couple of free tits were a fair price in exchange for a life of barely working and doing whatever she liked. "I didn't like working, every time I walked through the door I thought about quitting." She tells me that she reads and writes a lot, watches a ton of movies, and that she's a bit lonely but happy most of the time. And she tells me that sometimes she worries that she's just created her own narrative in order to avoid accepting that she's actually become a fickle woman and not the performance of a fickle woman, but she doesn't really care because she keeps doing her collages at home and selling them online, and when she needs money, she calls up one of her "friends" and says her boiler broke and her "friend" sends her a few hundred euros so she isn't cold. Most of the time, she has no regrets. She looks toward the playground and asks: "What does the body matter, Marisa?" She says the body is just a tool, like a painter's canvas or a sculptor's block of marble. And she asks me what I think.

"I don't know," I reply. We ask the waiter for another bottle of wine. "I feel like I'm constantly performing when I'm in the office."

"Life is a performance," affirms Elena, drunk.

"And I like to think that it's a game, that it's not contaminating me, that I go there every day but I'm still a migrating bird, that someday I'll quit that job and I can spit in Maika's mouth or leave a turd on her desk like that woman who won the lottery, but at the same time it seems impossible. I have the feeling there is no escape, that we're all condemned to play the role we've been assigned."

"Who's Maika?"

"A retard."

Elena laughs. "I don't think you can say that."

Night was starting to fall and the evening seemed like a distant dream, one where you're with someone familiar but they aren't exactly themselves. Like Elena. Physically she's changed, but her essence remains the same. I convey that idea to her in a vague, boozy way, and she nods. She repeats two or three times that she isn't a prostitute, that she wants to make that clear, but then she reminds me that we're feminists and it would be perfectly fine if she were one.

"You know how they say . . ." she reflects drunkenly, looking both at me and past me at a streetlight that just turned on, ". . . that 'It's a degrading profession' or 'Do you think they would do that if they didn't have to?' And I think, come on now, you fucking shit-for-brains, is it not degrading to walk up four floors to deliver a hamburger to an idiot? If you won the lottery, would you be going to work the next day?"

I tell her I understand. And then we tell each other how brilliant we are. We say we *have* to get together more often and toast to the performance of life, to being the greatest artists in the Western world, to being so devoted to our art that we're able to live it.

We leave when the waiter tells us the bar is closing and brings us the hefty bill. We've drunk three bottles of wine and we're completely wasted. Elena asks me where I live so she can take me home and get a cab from there. On the way to my house, I vomit between two parked cars while Elena holds my hair and tells me it's OK and I shouldn't worry because no one is passing by, although I see a man with a dog who mutters something like "Disgusting." When I manage to somewhat recover, we walk arm in arm to my apartment. I'm so drunk that Elena has to open it for me. I lie down in bed and Elena takes off my shoes and clothes and folds them meticulously on the chair. She goes to the bathroom and comes back with cotton pads and micellar water. I am putty in her hands. Elena silently removes my makeup, running the cotton pad gently over my eyelids, my forehead, my cheeks, my chin, and finally my neck. I smile.

"I saw a thread on Reddit the other day that was funny," I say with my eyes closed. "Imagine you're on vacation with your husband and suddenly he disappears, you call the police and spend the day searching for him with the authorities, and you get back to the hotel that night, tired, thinking your husband's probably dead. The next day you have to wake up very early to keep searching with the police . . . Would you do your skin care routine that night?"

"Of course I would," responds Elena.

"Me too." I smile with my eyes still closed; then I open them and observe her sitting on the edge of the bed, with her head tilted to one side, stroking my hair. "I'm afraid, Elena."

"Of what?"

"Of everyone forgetting about me."

"Nobody's going to forget you, Marisa."

Elena finishes combing my hair in silence. Then she leaves me a glass of water and an ibuprofen on the bedside table. I observe her silhouette in the doorway, Elena with her cell phone in her hand, probably calling a cab. She looks back at me and tells me to close my eyes. I nod, but I don't do it. A few minutes later, she leaves, closing the door carefully behind her.

I toss and turn in bed, trying to find a position where everything stops spinning, but it's impossible. I sit up slowly until I'm seated on the edge of the bed. I drink the glass of water and try not to puke. I take deep breaths. I'm still drunk, and I feel like if I stop moving, I'll die. You get to an age when getting wasted isn't fun anymore; it's an open portal to hell on earth. I don't even want to think about the hangover: that's a problem for future Marisa.

I get up and walk around my room. My heart is racing, but if I take an Ativan now, I'll wake up tomorrow feeling like I've been punched in the head. I think I can control it, to a certain extent. My brain is vomiting up the bile of all my negative self-talk. I'll always be alone. I'll never be happy. No one cares about me. No one knows who I really am. I'm an impostor, a professional fake, a master of deceit. That's why all my relationships fail. That's why they all leave. That's why nobody loves me. I feel enormous guilt for all the things that could've been done to avoid ending up in this situation, and also for all the things I did that put me here. I try to calm myself down. I wander around the bed, putting my right hand on my chest to stabilize myself. I imagine Elena's voice saying: "Everything will be fine, Marisa." And Elena's voice transforms, syllable by syllable, into Rita's voice. I know what's going on with me. I know why I can't calm down in here.

I walk to the closet. Inside, at the back, is the box of Rita's belongings, gathering dust since I brought it home. I knew this day would come, sooner or later. I pull it out delicately and bring it to the kitchen. I place it on the table and hold it with both hands. I feel like I'm about to perform an autopsy, and that idea makes me gag again. I take a deep breath and open the box. I start pulling things out and placing them on the table the way I've seen them do on shows like *CSI*. There is a person inside here. Or what's left of her.

Exhibit A: An eggplant-colored pashmina shawl that Rita always kept on the back of her chair because she said the air-conditioning gave her a chill. On the hottest days, Rita would wrap it around her neck and shoulders and stroll through the office as if she were a modern version of Marthe Keller in *Fedora*, without sunglasses but just as crazy. I bring it up to my face to see if it smells like her, but it doesn't smell like anything.

Exhibit B: A collection of twenty-four colored pencils, Faber-Castell brand. Hardly used.

Exhibit C: A framed image of a meme that Rita kept on her desk the way other people keep family photos. It comes from the episode of *The Simpsons* where Homer has to give up his dream job at the bowling alley and go back to the nuclear power plant because Marge is pregnant for the third time and he needs a better salary. In the final scene, his boss, the evil Mr. Burns, gives Homer a plaque that reads DON'T FORGET. YOU'RE HERE FOREVER. Homer covers up the message with different photos of his newborn daughter, until the remaining letters spell out DO IT FOR HER. Written over Maggie's face were the words "The paycheck."

Exhibit D: A small plastic carrying case with a toothbrush, toothpaste, and dental floss.

Exhibit E: A copy of *The Talented Mr. Ripley*, with a bookmark placed nearly at the end, which reminds me of the first time we sat in front of each other in the cafeteria.

Exhibit F: The mug I gave Rita, with the inscription "Your incompetency is not my emergency" in Comic Sans. It still has coffee stains. Maybe from the last coffee she ever drank.

Exhibit G: A black notebook. The black notebook that Rita brought to meetings and kept on her desk. I open it up and read her first notes: "Hand in mockup of Fritos Gourmet PPT: Friday 17. Client meeting energy drinks Tuesday 7 at 12:30 (Avenida de América). Meeting ideas day 5 campaign You Look Good Makeup: natural look, pastel colors but veering toward neutrals, girly design but not cheesy, inclusivity (use a black woman)."

I notice that Rita would often make little caricatures of people around the office. They're cute drawings, always in the margins, at the end of her meeting notes. There's a drawing of someone who is clearly Ramón, wearing an oversized suit and carrying a net kilo bag of tangerines, with a speech bubble that reads "The more we do, the more we can do." I smile. Another one looks like Fermín, a young guy who worked with Rita in the design department, and who always made disgustingly sexist comments without realizing how disgustingly sexist they were. Above him is the sentence "No, but I'd like to watch." I scowl. I flip through the first pages, trying to remember when we met, before we started sitting together at lunch every day.

I see several scathing caricatures of my coworkers until, finally, I find myself. That's me. That's my haircut; that's an outfit I could have worn to the office: a white blouse and cigarette pants with white Converse. Disguised as a creative, dressy but a touch casual. Disguised as a clown. My mini-me is holding a cell phone in her right hand and a little white box in her left. I read my speech bubble: "The day doesn't start until I take my first Ativan." I try to figure out when she drew that. Was it after our conversation in the cafeteria? If not, how did she know I was taking antianxiety meds? My mouth starts getting dry again. My caricature seems much crueler than the others, more personal, more hurtful, and also more accurate. Maybe because she knew me better. Maybe Rita was an asshole to everyone, including me. Maybe she didn't like me. Maybe she hated me. No. That's not possible. Maybe Rita was in worse shape than any of us thought, worse shape than any of us wanted to believe.

I flip through the pages, approaching August of last year. "Meeting Ramón, Monday 8th, 10:30 (in his office). Ideas meeting 10th, electric car campaign: neon, electric guitars, Bob Dylan, switch from analog to electric (due on the 29th). Lay out presentation robot vacuums: 16th. Meeting Let's Make It (event organizers), 14th, 11:30 (Cuzco)." Between those lines are scribbles, drawings, illustrations. A tiny devil in the right corner with a bubble that says "9 to 5." An office coffee machine with the drawing of a sunset on a paradisiacal beach and the message "Enjoy your 5 minutes." A drawing of her spot in the office, with her looking at her computer, and through the window where she'd contemplate the outside world is the Gran Vía in ruins with dinosaurs, zombies and humans trying to kill them, vampires, a Frankenstein monster, skaters, firemen, astronauts, Jesus Christ coming down from the heavens. There is nothing more after that. I guess that counts as a suicide note.

I wrap her pashmina shawl around my shoulders. I take her toiletry bag to my bathroom. I put her notebook and *The Tal-*

ented Mr. Ripley on my bedside table. I carefully place the rest of the objects back into the box. I close it and put it back in the closet. I drink another glass of water and take the ibuprofen. It's four in the morning. I lie down in bed, covered only by Rita's shawl. I pull my right leg out to touch the floor when the room starts spinning. A thought runs through my head, almost a fantasy: in *The Talented Mr. Ripley,* Tom Ripley murders and supplants the identity of a young multimillionaire who is living the bohemian life in southern Italy. Maybe Rita read the novel and decided to change her identity, to disappear, to fake her own death so she wouldn't have to explain herself.

I stroke the soft shawl while I fantasize about that possibility, until I realize that those things only happen in fiction. Real life is much more ordinary: metro rides, evenings at the supermarket, calls to your phone company's customer service, gynecological checkups, baskets of dirty clothes that pile up in the bathroom, toothpaste tubes that are squeezed and folded to get out the last drop, unanswered messages from people you want to answer and answered messages from people you couldn't care less about, bills, loyalty cards for La Sirena frozen foods and Carrefour accumulating in your wallet, dishcloths that smell damp, deep-cleaning the kitchen after a lot of frying. In real life, boredom exists, as does uneasiness and situations that lead to nothing, no character growth or plot advancement of any sort. Besides, how could she have pulled it off? And why? Wouldn't it have been easier to quit, take a break, and get a change of scenery? Nevertheless, the idea of Rita in another city with a different name gives me peace.

I flip through her drawings again. They become darker and more cryptic as August progresses. I go back to the beginning. To all those meeting notes, all those due dates. To all those projects she started and finished so she could start and finish others, like Sisyphus. Her days, after all, were so similar to mine . . . One day leads to the next. To the weekend. Then another whole week. On and on again, until they all blend together. Rita throwing herself onto the train tracks one hot August morning. People complaining because they'll be late for work. I hug Rita's shawl and feel enormous anguish. I feel like crying. There is no way that Rita is living in San Remo. I know this. I put Rita's notebook down, pick up my phone, and open YouTube. I put on a playlist of videos where rich celebrities lead tours through their homes. "Hello, I'm Gwyneth Paltrow, welcome to my house in Montecito, come on in!" I watch at least seven videos until the voices of rich American women start to have a calming effect on me. My heart slows. Sleep begins to envelop me. When I drop off to sleep, I can feel my face is damp with tears.

VIII

I wake up with my mouth bone-dry, and I grab my water as if it were a hand keeping me from falling into a black hole. Daylight slips through the window. My head is pounding and the light hurts my eyes. I don't know if I'm about to throw up. One of the things I miss about my twenties is the absence of hangovers. Being able to wake up fresh as a daisy and not wanting to fling myself off a cliff, even if I'd gone to sleep an hour before.

I pick up my phone and look at the time: it's 10:30. Natalia sent a WhatsApp message asking if I'm coming in today and saying she wants to discuss some things. I don't see any messages from the higher-ups. Luckily, it's still August. I write Natalia back: "Hello, Natalia. I can't come in today, last night I ate something that didn't sit well with me." Natalia immediately replies. "Oh, you poor thing! What happened? Can I do anything?" What happened is that I drank all of Madrid and part of Toledo, Natalia. What happened is I puked between two cars and someone had to get me home and into bed. What happened is I got together with a friend, and it's been a long time since I could say that. And not just any old friend, not a boring, ordinary person, but a fascinating, cultured, highly intelligent, and absolutely beautiful woman who decided to get a boob job to get money out of old men and not have to work in an office and answer questions from people like you. "I don't know, I ordered sushi, something must have been off," I write. Poor Natalia.

I lower the blinds to turn my bedroom into a cave; I shake out the sheets, turn on the air-conditioning, brush my teeth, and lie back down. I think about how my to-do list seemed so doable yesterday: it's Thursday, so I still have one day to finish my part of the Christmas campaign and organize my talk for the retreat. I can rest for a couple more hours and then get started. I open YouTube, my salvation. It suggests a knitting tutorial. It's forty-five minutes long. I hit play. Our teacher is an adorable woman with graying hair and loud clothes. The town kook. I smile. I lie on my side while she explains knitting, and little by little, in her company, I enter into a calm sleep.

I open my eyes several hours later. It's ten minutes after four and I'm hungry. On YouTube, it's the same woman in another, even louder sweater. I open a food-delivery app and order a rotisserie chicken. I stand up and go take a shower. If I didn't have to work, these hangovers wouldn't hurt so much. I hate having to be a functional person when I just want to collapse like a rag doll. Our bodies just need time to recover, be it from the worst accident or the worst hangover or the worst breakup. I feel myself coming back to life under the cool water of the shower. I get out, dry off, and put on clean clothes. I let my hair air-dry. I smear myself with lotion. My food arrives and I serve it on the kitchen table. I grab my laptop, and while I eat, I organize ideas for the Christmas campaign.

I open Natalia's PowerPoint. As always, it's perfect—she has clearly put a lot of time and energy into it. I scroll through it like an automaton, just reading the phrases in bold. Women buy fewer gifts now, but they spend more on the ones they do buy. There is a growing trend toward buying yourself gifts. It is very important to be situated as a "top-of-mind" brand. Things labeled as "luxury" sell better during Christmas because people feel they have a right to treat themselves. In Spain, a lot of people give gifts on Christmas, but the bigger gift-giving is still on Three Kings' Day. The most popular Christmas present is still perfume. All this information is depressing: adults buying impersonal, meaningless products; adults buying products to fill voids; adults buying things to show other adults they care about them, measuring that affection in their prices. I send an email to Natalia saying that it all looks very good and that soon I'll send her ideas to include in the presentation. I start with the ideas my students came up with. It's obvious they put in effort because they always put in effort. My job is figuring out which ones, besides putting in the effort, hit upon a decent enough idea that could be useful to me.

I look at the first PowerPoint. Perfume, lipstick, lotion for women over forty, and an eye shadow palette. The first slide asks "WHAT DO WOMEN WANT?" The second slide responds "TO FEEL UNIQUE AND SPECIAL." I scowl. Student 1 suggests a creative strategy whose main idea is "BE THE WOMAN YOU WANT TO BE, NOT THE ONE THEY TELL YOU TO BE." It wouldn't be half bad if it wasn't like nine hundred other ads. As if women were snakes or hermit crabs who could shed our skin on a whim and find another one.

I open up a Word document from student 2. It's a list of ideas for each product. I rule them all out except for ideas on the face cream for women over forty: "Yes! I'm over forty!" Student 2's tactic is to encourage feeling pride about your age and quit hiding it. It could be a good starting point. "Yes! My hangovers now last three days!" "Yes! My period is starting to be irregular!"

"Yes! Every guy I sleep with assumes I'm looking for a stable relationship!" "Yes! My tits are starting to sag!" Why not.

Student 3 sent a PowerPoint in dark tones where the buzz-words are "passion," "desire," and "night." I copy and paste a phrase: "I'm more myself when I like what I see in the mirror."

Student 4 sent a thirty-seven-page manifesto about impossible beauty standards and the need for companies to be more honest about what they're selling. I hope with all my heart that student finds a job that has nothing to do with advertising. I steal a few lines from her.

I open another email: "The revolution is inside you." Another one: "We need you to make the most of your natural beauty." Another: "This is all you need to be yourself." It seems these fresh young minds have a common denominator: they've bought into the new message of using cosmetic products to feel empowered, and that you're doing it for yourself and not for others.

I look at the time and realize I've spent two hours reading their emails and now have a four-page document. I copy and paste the most interesting and attention-grabbing phrases into a Word document, edit them to seem written by the same person and not by twenty teenagers on speed. I look for synonyms that sound better, expressions that are closer to what clients usually like. I give shape to the document so that it sounds halfway decent. I feel like Elizabeth Báthory, who went down in history as "the Blood Countess" because she drank the blood of young girls hoping to remain forever young. Or maybe I'm like one of those aliens in a sci-fi, sucking the brains out of the youth to acquire universal knowledge. Or maybe I'm not a monster at all; maybe I'm just the result of a life of work, another human being maintaining the status quo out of pure laziness, and now I appropriate other people's ideas the way older people used to appropriate mine. Maybe I'm just another stagnant adult who's lost the energy to change things. Something that, come to think of it, might make me the worst sort of monster.

I start a new email and copy in Natalia and the rest of the team on vacation. Being in middle management means starting things, delegating them, and then supervising them. It's about making it seem like you're much busier than you really are and knowing how to stay firm when your superiors point out a screwup by one of your underlings. It's being a wall, but I'd rather deal with Maika's animosity one day than have to stay until midnight on a Tuesday debating whether the slogan "Yes, I'm forty!" is better than "I love being forty." I write:

Dear team,

I've been working on the creative approaches and key points for our Christmas campaign. I'm attaching a document with everything I've come up with so you can begin developing it. Set up a weekly status meeting so I can see how it is progressing.

Natalia, add your insights at the beginning of the presentation, they're very interesting and could be inspiring for your colleagues.

I send the email and close my laptop as forcefully as if I'd found child porn on it. It's 6:30 and I'm no longer hungover. I make myself a coffee and go out to the terrace. I have a message from Elena asking how I'm doing. "I literally only started being functional as a human 5 minutes ago," I respond. Elena answers immediately: "Hahaha, we must do that again." I think about Elena and about Pablo, and the viral image of a mural featuring Britney Spears lyrics comes to mind. The first was from ". . . Baby One More Time": "My loneliness is killing me." Underneath that is a line from "Stronger": "Loneliness ain't killing me no more." I often think about that mural. I often think about Britney Spears. I think about all the times we feel lonely until someone shows up, when you least expect it, to make you feel like part of something. As if you've finally reached Ithaca.

Madrid is gleaming blue, and that puts me in a good mood. You'll never see bluer skies than in August, when the Madrileños leave and stop polluting the air with their cars. I think of places I could go on vacation when everybody else comes back from theirs, and the only thing I think to look for are places without a lot of cars and where there's the possibility of a starry sky. I go onto a flight app. I type in my dates and scroll through potential destinations. I like the idea of my vacation being determined by an algorithm. I don't want to get up early, so I choose only flights after ten in the morning, and I don't want to fly with a low-cost airline because they make you feel like cattle on the way to the slaughterhouse. My options shift. Life, in the end, is a lot like a search engine: as you make decisions, your options get fewer, until you have to choose between two or three and pray you haven't made a mistake. They don't have the option for a starry sky, so now I have to be my own algorithm. An island. I see Mallorca, I see Sicily, I see Fuerteventura. Of those three, there's only one I've never been to. I book a round trip to Fuerteventura and I start to imagine myself there, but the idea is fuzzy because I haven't the slightest clue of what Fuerteventura looks like. I search for photos of the island. It looks gorgeous. I see a long beach covered in dunes and a little inland town that is tinted white.

The doorbell rings and I jump. I'm not expecting any packages, so I stay on my terrace trying not to make a sound. I look at more photos: beaches, towns, typical dishes. The doorbell rings again. A few seconds later, my phone screen lights up with Pablo's name.

"Hello?" I answer, whispering.

"Are you at home?" asks Pablo, who is whispering now too.

"Yes," I say almost inaudibly.

"So why won't you answer the door?" he replies, in a normal tone now.

"Because I wasn't expecting anyone," I say, approaching the door, through which I can now hear Pablo on the other side.

"And what if it was a neighbor asking for help?"

"That kind of thing doesn't happen anymore, Pablo."

"Well, are you?"

"Am I what?"

"Are you going to let me in or not?"

I hang up and open the door. "What a surprise! Have you been waiting long?"

Pablo rolls his eyes. He has his phone in one hand and a six-pack of beer in the other. He walks past me with hardly a glance and puts the beer in the fridge.

"What were you doing?" he asks as he sticks two cans into the freezer. "What was the oh-so-important task I've had the audacity to interrupt?"

"I was buying tickets for a trip to Fuerteventura next week."

Pablo taps the rest of the six-pack to see which ones are coldest and grabs one for each of us.

"Did we have plans to hang out tonight?"

"No, but I felt like having a beer, and drinking alone seems like something a borderline depressive does. Do you mind?"

I shake my head. Pablo opens his beer and takes a long drink; I do the same.

"Fuerteventura?"

"Yeah, I've never been," I say.

"Me either. You going alone?"

"Yeah, why? You want to come?"

Pablo drinks again, studying me. He seems to be gauging whether my offer is real or just one of our jokes and, in the case it's real, he's weighing whether us spending a week alone together in Fuerteventura is a good idea. I don't know the answer to either question.

"Should we go out on the terrace?" I say to avoid breaking our equilibrium.

"OK."

We sit on the terrace. Beer takes the place of my coffee, and I realize that it's doing more for my hangover than the rotisserie chicken and the coffee did. A YouTuber once said that hangovers were dehydration plus withdrawal, so the best thing you can do, according to that twenty-five-year-old with zero medical training, is keep drinking the next day.

Pablo pats his pockets in search of his cigarettes. When he finds them, he gives me one without asking. He lights his; he lights mine.

"I think I have a lot going on at work next week," says Pablo, looking out at infinity to avoid looking at me.

What he really means is what I'm thinking too: "It would be a little weird, wouldn't it?" or "Are you sure? Is that a good idea?" or "What if our relationship only works on your terrace?"

"I can check, maybe I could come on the weekend or something like that."

"Great. You let me know," I respond without the slightest hint of anger or bitterness. When I take a drag, I feel a bit dizzy, so I stub it out and take another sip of beer. "I recently watched a documentary about a house in Fuerteventura I want to visit. You have to call up the owner ahead of time so he can pick you up at a certain part of the island because there are no roads where the house is."

"And what is it about that house?"

"It's called Casa Winter and, according to the rumors, it belonged to the Nazis."

Pablo stops staring out into infinity and looks at me.

"It was built in 1946 and belonged to a German named Gustav Winter. The house is hidden, in the middle of nowhere—it's crazy they could even get it built in those days. And why would someone build a fortress in the middle of nowhere? A German someone."

"To hide," responds Pablo, turning his torso toward me.

"Exactly."

"Are you going to visit it?"

"I'd like to, sure."

"Who does it belong to now?"

"I don't know, some guy."

"And you're going to meet up with some guy you don't know from Adam so he can take you to a Nazi house in the middle of nowhere?"

"When you put it that way, it sounds like a Tinder date."

Pablo laughs.

"I think he charges 10 euros, or something like that, to show the house."

"He could at least have the decency to buy you a drink first." Pablo laughs at his own joke and I join in. "But is this guy a Nazi?"

"No, I don't think he's a Nazi, but I can ask when I get there."

"You can't ask someone if they're a Nazi, can you? It's, like, impolite. You'll have to be very subtle about it."

"Subtle like how? I can't see myself saying, 'What a lovely spot, it makes one feel like a superman; do you feel like a superman?'"

"You can ask if he has any tattoos that don't allow him to enter Germany."

"Yeah, very subtle," I respond. "I'll think about it."

"What else are you planning to do there?"

"I don't know." I shrug. "Swim in the sea, eat fresh fish, sleep."

"That's a good plan."

We drink and look out at the horizon. Pablo stretches and leans back in his chair. We are enveloped in silence, but it's no longer uncomfortable. Nothing like a good Nazi mystery to break the ice. I think how we could be just like this on some beach in Fuerteventura, but I don't dare suggest it again, and I'm somewhat sad to feel that inexplicable fear of Pablo's rejection.

"Who was that girl last night?" asks Pablo suddenly.

"What girl?"

"That girl you tried to get into my apartment with."

I look at him blankly.

"You don't remember? Last night, totally wasted, you were trying to unlock my door for ten minutes, I opened it, you were with a girl, and I told her you lived in the apartment upstairs. I walked you up here, opened the door for you, and she thanked me, then she said she didn't need anything more from men, not then and not ever."

I let out a hearty laugh. Definitely something Elena would say—the story must be true.

"All that really happened?" I ask, shocked that I'd blacked out.

Pablo and Elena coinciding in the same point in space and time, and I had erased such an important moment from my memory. Last night, when Elena and I were drinking, I think I told her about Pablo. Or maybe I just thought about telling her about him. I imagined how I would introduce them: "And you are my best friends in the entire world." Now I'm kind of embarrassed to have come up with such a childish intro. Maybe it's better they met the way they did, saving the inevitable uncomfortable formalities of a first meeting.

"Yes."

"Elena, my best friend."

"What do you mean, your best friend? Quit messing with me," says Pablo, both surprised and amused.

"I'm not messing with you."

"How can she be your best friend when you've never talked about her and I've never met her?"

"You met her yesterday."

This didn't seem to convince him. He shoots me a defiant look.

"Because we ran into each other after a long time."

"When?"

"Yesterday."

"What does she do?"

"What does that matter? Why is everyone always so interested in what people do for a living?"

"Well, OK, how do you know each other?"

"From university, we were inseparable, like white on rice." I give Pablo a brief summary of our friendship in school: how we met, what we used to do, what bars we went to and what movies we watched, a few amusing anecdotes and a couple cringey ones, but enough information to convince him that Elena is, truly, someone in my life and not just a complete stranger who put me to bed last night. "And I don't think I've felt that way with anyone since."

I get a notification on my phone. Pablo sees the screen light up with a reminder that reads "Call dealer." He again looks confused. I tell him about the team-building retreat and how I need drugs to get through an entire weekend surrounded by people I hate. He doesn't seem judgmental; he seems to understand. He says he has some marijuana and a few bags left over from parties. Molly, probably. A lot of pills. I tell him that will work, and he goes to his place to bring me the stash. Later Pablo helps me find an Airbnb in Fuerteventura while we complain about the enormous damage Airbnb is causing to cities.

The sky starts to turn pink and then purple, and before it's even nine p.m., my head starts to nod with sleepiness. Pablo offers to order some pizzas, but I tell him I'm not hungry, that he can eat some of the chicken if he wants. He doesn't try to spend the night. He throws away the empty cans and leaves. I brush my teeth and wash my face, smear on some lavender night cream that sells the promise of eternal youth, put on a clean nightgown, and go to bed. I fall asleep listening to an old Televisión Española program about the whistled language of La Gomera island.

IX

I wake up with my heart racing. Friday is usually my favorite day, when the long workweek is ending but the weekend is still filled with possibilities, but this Friday is just the beginning of a weekend with people from work. I shower, dress, have a coffee and an Ativan, and think of how I can possibly fake being someone who is genuinely interested in the latest series someone watched, and therefore not deserving of being fired. I stick a bunch of clothes I won't wear into a small suitcase, plus my toiletry bag and the fanny pack filled with Pablo's drugs.

I google "how to be creative" and find a BuzzFeed listicle with tips. "Always carry a notebook," it says. "Sing in the shower." "Drink coffee." "Get up early." "Listen to new music." What a crock of shit. I go into YouTube and type "how to be creative ted talk." It offers me a super long list of videos featuring middle-aged men reviewing self-help books on creativity that were published by big houses. I sense that the first tip is to buy yourself a linen shirt and a garish pair of glasses. On the way to the retreat, I'll put together a PowerPoint with a mishmash of ideas that I can riff off of for forty-five minutes. I'll look up a title that will sound clever to people who don't spend time on the internet, like "The Seven Deadly Sins of Creativity" or "Being Creative Is Easy if You Know How."

I head out for the office, trusting that today, more than ever, I'll get hit by a bus. Pros of being hit by a bus today: I wouldn't have to deal with the team-building retreat. Cons of getting hit by a bus today: I wouldn't get to go to Fuerteventura. Pros: Medical leave. Cons: What if I'm left mentally disabled? Pros: I could read all the volumes of Proust's *In Search of Lost Time.* Cons: I wouldn't get to see the Nazi house. I decide to let luck choose my fate.

I open up Spotify and allow myself to be carried off by the music. I turn up the volume until I can no longer hear the sounds of the city. A song from the eighties comes on, called "En cualquier fiesta" by La Mode. I listen carefully while I wait for the light to turn green. "Cuando todo se acabe y nadie nos recuerde seguro que nos vemos en cualquier fiesta." *When everything's over and no one remembers us, we'll probably meet up at some random party.* I cross when I'm supposed to. I walk with quick, light steps. I think about Pablo, I think about Elena, I think about Rita, and I feel a stab of sadness. I observe the office at the end of the street; there are already people gathering in the doorway, waiting for the private bus that will drive us to hell.

I approach that absurd group of people united by a common bond: not having enough money to not be there. Ramón is dressed as if he were Coronel Tapiocca himself. I see Carlos, the forty-five-year-old chief financial officer who would have been attractive if his life weren't played out on a Monopoly board. Mentxu and Sonsoles, from HR. I'm not sure which one is Mentxu and which one is Sonsoles. They're interchangeable, using the same expressions from the same generic email account, as if work had fused them into a single being, a photocopy of a photocopy, created one dark night in 1970 and beamed out in ultraviolet light into this very office. People named Carlos, people named Borja, people named Virginia or Lourdes whom you occasionally coincide with in meetings, in cafés near the office, at company dinners, in elevators and stairwells, and whom you greet in a friendly way and ask how they're doing, but you know that if they'd committed some horrific crime and you had to come up with an identifying trait for each of them, you wouldn't be able to. This is why everyone always ends up saying the murderer in their apartment building was always friendly. And at the back, Maika, on her phone, looking like a supervillain. She gives me an alarmed expression while she exhales cigarette smoke into the air.

"Are you OK, Marisa?" asks Sonsoles or Mentxu.

"Of course, why?"

"You're crying."

I furrow my brow and raise a hand to my cheek. It's true, I am crying. Note to self: don't listen to music that transports you to a tragic alternate universe before nine in the morning.

"Oh, that's nothing." I wipe away the tears. "It's the pollution."

Sonsoles or Mentxu looks at me somewhat suspiciously, but she doesn't dare say anything. I put my bag down and glance around. Suddenly I am fully aware that I possess a body and need to do something with it, but I don't know what to do with my limbs and I don't know what to do with all this corporeal presence.

"It looks like we're almost all here, right?" Sonsoles or Mentxu crosses my name off a list.

"Still waiting on five people, that's fine, we're still on time." She says "on time" in English.

Sonsoles or Mentxu smiles. I smile. I wonder at what moment in our evolution we decided that it would make us seem more intelligent and cosmopolitan to say certain words in English.

"The bus isn't leaving for another half hour."

"Ahh!" Shoot me now.

We smile at each other again. Is she as uncomfortable as I am? Is she also screaming inside at the thought of a weekend of one awkward silence after another and endless elevator conversations?

"I saw that you're taking vacation days next week, right?" she says, lowering her little folder. "So lucky, I love going out of town in September when everything's not so crowded."

"Yeah! Me too," I respond politely, grateful that she's filling the silence.

"And where are you going?" she asks affably.

"I'm going to Fuerteventura."

"Oh, how wonderful, I was there with my boyfriend during Easter Week. If you need recommendations, I can send you an email."

"Sure, that'd be fantastic, because I have no idea what I'm going to do there."

"Are you going alone?"

"Yeah, but I have two friends who are living there now," I lie. "They're painters."

"How interesting."

"Yeah, and lesbians," I add.

"Then you probably don't need my recommendations."

"No, no, send them to me anyway so I can surprise them."

"I know of several nudist beaches and coves, although really most of the beaches there have nude sections."

"Oh, that's cool," I say, now thinking about Sonsoles or Mentxu swimming buck naked and not entirely sure where this conversation is headed.

"Yeah, we stayed in a nudist town," she continues, squinting at a person in the distance until she determines they aren't one of our flock and looks at me again. "We always try to vacation in nudist spots, it's the only way to get a break from your cell phone."

I'm speechless. I guess this is the pleasant version of finding out your friendly neighbor is actually a serial killer. This person behind rimless glasses and the hairstyle of a nineties actress summers in nudist colonies. You never really know people. Reception areas, hallways, and landings certainly don't encourage deep conversations.

"And since when have you been nudists?"

"Oof, years. We actually met on a nudist beach."

"And that wasn't tricky?"

"What?"

"No, I just mean . . ." I stammer, trying not to mention the fact that, the day she met her boyfriend, without even three drinks first, she saw his penis. "Meeting someone on a nude beach," I say pragmatically.

"Well, it saves you some disappointments," she says with a naughty smile. What an elegant way to tell me her boyfriend is packing heavy artillery. I let out a laugh. "Speaking of nudism, did you bring your bathing suit? There's a spa in the hotel."

"Yeah, I brought one," I respond, amazed at her easy change of subject. I still don't know if I'm talking to Sonsoles or to Mentxu, but whoever it is, she's just become my favorite person on this trip.

"I'm excited. I'm sure we'll have fun and learn a lot," she says with the smile of the old Sonsoles or Mentxu, the one who worships the aseptic office environment and venerates work and service contracts. "Here comes the bus, talk to you later, Marisa."

"Mentxu!" shouts Maika from a distance.

I take note of her name: Mentxu. It's odd, I would've bet my left hand she was Sonsoles.

We line up obediently and, gradually, after leaving our luggage in the compartment, take our seats on the bus. I get a window seat and begin to feel the tranquilizer I took this morning.

Carlos, chief financial officer, asks if he can sit next to me, and I generously place my bag at my feet. Of course you can sit next to me, Carlos the *chief financial officer.* I adore your lack of interest in our lives, your moderation, your silence, your indifference to anything that isn't about money. You are the best travel companion I could wish for.

Five seconds after sitting down, Carlos starts looking at his cell phone. I wonder if I might be happier married to someone like Carlos, a regular guy, a bit boring, but whom I could ask what he wanted for dinner on Mondays after work before going to the supermarket. Someone I could binge-watch some Netflix series with, whose plot we'd forget after a couple of weeks, and someone I could eat out with on Friday nights at a restaurant that's no more than 80 euros a head, but never less than 50. Someone who went out every Sunday morning to ride his bicycle through Madrid Río Park with his group of middle-aged buddies, while I stayed home doing the laundry with nary a thought beyond the clothes coming out very clean and lavender-scented. A simple life, not tragic in the least, mortally routine, moderately happy.

Maybe some people's problem—and by "some people," I mean me—is that we think life is going to offer us something extraordinary when we least expect it. One day we'll stumble across our smidgen of luck, and from then on, we'll be happy, because everything around us will change without us having to lift a finger.

No more Ativan for breakfast, no more empty feeling when you arrive home. No more unexpected weeping when you see a Coca-Cola ad; no more taking walks through the city hoping to find something that never finds you. That indeterminate but grandiose something that, in fact, more than finding you, seems to be fleeing from you.

I rest my forehead on the window and watch Madrid vanish.

Maybe that's the secret to happiness, lowering your expectations, settling, playing paddle tennis, making paella on Sundays, having a group of girlfriends, getting your manicure done every fifteen days, having kids, recycling, adopting a dog, moving to the suburbs, having a garden, marrying Carlos.

"Are you married, Carlos?"

Carlos glances up from his cell phone and stares at me.

"Yes," he says, and lowers his gaze back to whatever he was doing.

"Wow, congratulations."

"Thanks."

I sleep the whole way. When I wake up, leaning on Carlos's shoulder, we are driving on an unpaved road through a forest that leads us to the hotel. The hotel has the kind of beauty typical of lodgings whose days of splendor are long past. We stretch and get off the bus. A group of very smiling bellhops asks us our names and takes us and our luggage to our rooms. Mentxu tells us to meet in the hotel lobby wearing comfortable shoes and athletic clothing. And I feel both curiosity and fear at the idea of seeing all my coworkers dressed in comfortable shoes and athletic clothing.

My room has a wooden framed window that overlooks a lovely tree-filled garden with mountains in the distance. I like hotel rooms because they allow you to live out the fantasy of being someone else for a couple of nights. In this tastefully decadent room in ocher tones and fine hardwoods, I can be whomever I feel like being. I run my hand over the soft cotton sheets tucked tightly beneath the bedspread; then I look through the bedside tables to see if someone left behind hidden treasure, but there is only a pamphlet on the hotel's recreational activities. Hotels used to always have Bibles in the bedside drawers, as if they wanted to remind you that, whatever you do, you'll be held accountable by God. I go into the bathroom, an oasis of white marble, and look through the amenities: a rose-scented body lotion, shower gel, shampoo and conditioner. Only good hotels remember the conditioner. Hotels for poor people assume that broke women enjoy having frizzy hair. I turn on the shower to check the water pressure and imagine the moment when I can spend two hours in there.

I go back into the room, open the minibar, and take a sip of a little bottle of vodka. Ah, that's nice. I could be a businesswoman with two kids and a slight drinking problem. Or a married man's lover waiting patiently in the refuge his secretary chose. I allow myself a few seconds of fantasizing as I look out at the trees before returning to reality. I open my bag and put on some leggings and a black T-shirt, and I lace up some old Nikes I bought back when I thought I'd start jogging and never did. Dread. A slight burst of anxiety. I use my last five minutes of pleasure and solitude to roll a joint and stick it in my fanny pack.

In the lobby, I find my coworkers disguised as people they aren't. Their hoodies and sporty sunglasses make them look like an AI portrait of several wanted people, or an incredibly lost gang of ravers from the nineties. Gray cotton sweatpants, Lycra neon leggings, shorts, multicolored sneakers. It's unnatural to see them like this; it's even embarrassing, like running into a teacher outside of school. Mentxu, my new best friend, the nudist, gives me a military vest that's too big and a bag that I have to tie around my wrist with a ribbon. My ribbon is red. I look around. Carlos has a blue ribbon. Ramón also has a blue one. Maika's is red.

"OK, have you ever played paintball?" says Mentxu.

My coworkers smile nervously. I wonder if it's too early to start taking drugs. Twenty people wearing military vests in the lobby of a luxury hotel in Segovia, it looks like we're about to commit a terrorist attack.

"This is the first surprise of the day!"

Mentxu and a couple of monitors lead us outside the hotel.

Most of us are walking in small groups, but without exchanging any words. A narrow dirt path leads us to a lush forest. Someone breaks the ice. "Mmmm . . . smells like the countryside." "Fill your lungs, feels so good." "Fresh air, amazing." "Man needs to have more contact with nature." "Living in Madrid is a trap." Laughter. I walk in silence within the group, but I don't feel a part of it. It's so easy for some people to connect, join in, participate. They feel so comfortable with the reiteration of ideas and superficial communication. I feel like a confused alien who's just landed on Earth. Twenty city mice, dressed like clowns, addicted to their cell phones, who can't even remember you can hail a cab by waiting on the curb and lifting an arm, talking about the transformative power of nature, less than seventy kilometers from Madrid, on an organized trip with every second of its twenty-four hours planned out. Humanity is like an enormous experiment.

I take a deep breath and watch the sun slipping through the branches of trees that could be pine, chestnut, almond, or ash—I don't know because I'm a city mouse too, but at least I'm not trying to pretend I'm not.

"This is a good place." The group stops short and looks at Ramón, who has begun speaking. "Team, before we begin the day's events, I'd like us to take a minute to think about our beloved colleague Rita, who passed away a year ago."

No way. I look around at my coworkers, who swap out their goofy smiles for solemn nods and ceremonious lowerings of their chins. Their relaxed postures straighten up in a sign of respect; those wearing hats remove them. A circle starts to form in the middle of the forest, with Ramón as master of ceremonies in the center, dressed like a Boy Scout troop leader.

"If anyone would like to say a few words . . ." Ramón looks at us each one by one, inviting us to share a memory, an anecdote, some kind words, and yet he finds a wall of silence.

He's caught us off guard, dressed in leggings and military

vests, thinking about shooting each other. What can we say in this uncomfortable interlude between our Roman games devoted, thanks to the gracious stylings of Ramón and the HR department, to the somber subject of death?

"Although there's no obligation . . ."

An increasingly larger, denser, more uncomfortable silence fills the forest. We all sense, for the first time since we left Madrid, how noisy nature can be when no one wants to speak.

"Rita was . . ." It's Mentxu who speaks, and we all look at her with gratitude, especially Ramón. "Rita was a very special person." She smiles kindly; everyone nods.

"Very, yes. She was a self-starter," someone murmurs.

A self-starter. A go-getter. Very smart. Imagine dying and all someone can think to say about you is that you were a "self-starter."

"And I think we all remember moments we shared with her," continues Mentxu, fully immersed in her role as perfect HR employee who can handle uncomfortable situations, like firing someone when they return from maternity leave, or deaths on the job. "I think we should each take this minute to think about those moments with her, here in this incomparable setting."

"I think that's a wonderful idea," says Ramón with relief. "OK . . ." He sighs and lifts his gaze to the heavens, indicating that the minute of silence has just started.

I glance at the paintball monitors, who are observing us from a prudent distance, with expressions of someone attending the funeral of a great-aunt they barely knew. I observe the group I have the shit luck of being part of: the more dramatic ones, like Ramón, are looking up at the sky. Others, probably atheists, have their gaze fixed on the ground. No one looks around; it would be like seeing each other naked.

One minute, that's all she gets. Sixty seconds. Sixty thousand milliseconds to remember a person who devoted eight hours of her day, forty hours a week, forty-eight weeks a year, during almost two years of her life to these people who actually hated her and have nothing to say about her. All our working lives are worth is a minute of silence in the middle of a recreational weekend.

What would Rita make of all this? I suppose right now she'd just be glad not to be here. This could reaffirm her idea of throwing herself onto the train tracks, of eating big spoonfuls of the rat poison she kept in a box under the sink, or of turning her computer off one day and never turning it back on again. She'd find it pathetic, false, even amoral. Being remembered out of obligation, cautiousness, because of what someone might say. Almost logistically, something to cross off a list. I sigh and look up at the sky too, exchanging one of those glances that only she and I understood.

How cringey. I'd like to ask any of these emotionally challenged people for a memory they have of Rita. A sincere, honest, real memory. I'd like someone to be capable of saying out loud that they once ripped her a new one for refusing to take on a task that wasn't hers to do. I'd like someone to recall how they used to sideline her in the cafeteria, because they thought she was an asshole for not wanting to work through her lunch break. I'd like to spit in all of their faces, insult them, scratch them and tell them they are pieces of shit who brought another human being to the point of total depletion, to depression, to taking her own life.

"OK," says Ramón. Everyone seems relieved that the two-hour-long minute is over. "Thank you, everyone."

The monitors approach us like someone approaching the survivors of a plane crash. Are you all right? Are you in one piece? Still got all your limbs? Come on, let's go. Leave the dead buried and let the living play paintball. I'm incapable of processing how my coworkers can change registers so quickly.

They lead us deeper into the forest, into a clearing with pallets, holes for people to hide in, even trenches. I will admit that I've imagined shooting a lot of the folks in my company, although I never thought it would be materialized. Maybe that's the game's real objective: being able to shoot at your boss in jest so you can draw on that memory every time he calls you after work asking you to solve some screwup. They hand us helmets and explain the rules: two teams, the winner is the one that remains the cleanest.

"The one tip I'd give you," says a monitor, "is that aim is as important as strategy in this game." I wonder how many times he's repeated this same song and dance, weekend after weekend, to people who look like us. "You have to trust and listen to your coworkers to beat the other team. Remember not to shoot at the eyes or head." Unbelievable. "You can move and talk freely. The game starts when you hear my whistle."

The red group and the blue group walk in opposite directions. My group forms a huddle where Maika, of course, is the one calling the shots.

"OK, I've got an idea," she says, peeking at the blue group. "Let's go for Carlos, Jorge, and Benito first, since they're the strongest. If we finish them off, it'll be easier to get the rest. We can go in groups of three, who's with me?" Maika looks at us one by one. "Marisa, you do Pilates, right?"

"I used to," I respond. I feel like I'm in *Full Metal Jacket,* except wearing old Oysho leggings.

"Well, better than nothing. You and José Luis can come with me and we'll go after Carlos. The rest of you decide how to deal with the other two. Then we'll all get together and decide who we'll exterminate next."

"Let's go, team," says one of us, putting his hand in the center of the huddle.

"Yeah, go, team!" shouts another.

"Let's go get 'em!" exclaims another.

We place our hands together just before the whistle sounds. Everyone disperses as if they were very clear on what they needed to do. Maika and José Luis hide behind an enormous wooden pallet. Maika waves me over. I squat down and hide with them. José Luis starts making those weird hand signals you see hunters doing in documentaries, and they start to squat walk. I follow them. A ball of blue paint whizzes past me, close but no cigar. I'm counting on getting shot as soon as possible so I can be out of the game. Now we're running through the forest, now we're hiding behind a tree, now we're kneeling, now we're standing again. It's exhausting. I can feel the vodka shot swirling in my stomach. Maika gives a warning.

"The bird is in the nest."

I nod as if I understand. Everyone suddenly seems to know military jargon. At Maika's yell, we stand up and run. I don't know where we're running to or who we're pursuing. All of a sudden, between two wooden pallets, we see Carlos. Carlos sees us and shoots. Maika shoots, José Luis shoots, I shoot too. Carlos is covered in paint and puts his arms up in surrender.

"Well played, guys," he says with a wide smile. "At least I took one of you with me." José Luis is down. And then we were eighteen.

Maika screams, runs, howls, and barks orders at me. I follow her instructions like a good—and terrified—girl. I confirm my theory that I would be the first to die if Spain went to war or a zombie apocalypse happened. I shoot on her order, I run on her order, I squat on her order. Maika says that we have to find our group because there's strength in numbers. I nod, and she runs like a hare from its den, but I remain stock-still behind a pallet.

I feel a disconnect between body and mind: I'm robotically following Maika's instructions, but my mind is completely blank, hoping to forget any traumatic memories of my coworkers running around and screaming. Maybe I'm the problem and not them. Maybe I should be capable of enjoying this, as ridiculous as it seems. I look around. Maika is calling me from somewhere, but I've vanished from her field of view. I hear more screaming in the distance, as if the battle were being fought somewhere far away. I'm alone, finally. I unclench all my muscles, stretch out my legs, and rest my back on the pallet. I pull the joint out of my fanny pack and light it up. Why? I couldn't tell you. Maybe it's not the best idea, but I don't care. Nothing going on around me makes any sense.

I take a couple of drags and look out at the forest and think of the phrase "can't see the forest for the trees." I think about how absurd it is to take a minute of silence for a dead person barely fifteen minutes before shooting paintballs at each other. I think about the drawing Rita made of me, the one that said my day doesn't start until I take my first Ativan. I bring my hand to my chest and I feel my heart racing. I search for the blister to calm my nerves, but I realize that I must have left it in the hotel. My dripping sweat suddenly freezes, I can't control my hands, and my legs wouldn't respond if I tried to run. But run where? Why? I observe my coworkers' helmets bobbing in the distance as they scream, and I realize that I've finally reached the third panel of the Hieronymus Bosch triptych. With no Rita, no Ativan, and no escape.

I stub out the joint and put it back in my bag. My mouth has gone completely dry, but I'd have to go onto the battlefield to find something to drink. I look up at the sky again, trying to control my breathing, and I wonder if, from now on, every time I look up at the sky through the treetops, I will remember that stupid minute of silence. I feel tears on my cheeks again. I think about my mother's call, every Tuesday at 6:15, and for a moment, I wish that it were Tuesday at 6:15 so I could tell her the whole truth: "Mom, I don't think I'm doing OK. I don't think anyone is entirely OK, but I think I'm a little worse than the rest. I don't think I'm as bad as a girl I knew, named Rita, who I never told you about, but who I think killed herself. Or maybe she didn't. Goes to show you how well I knew her. Mom, I want to escape, I don't want to be here, I don't want to live this life. Mom, I want to come back home, I want to go to sleep at ten every night and take walks and not have to make an effort to be someone." My pulse slows. By imagining a conversation with my mother, I managed to calm myself down enough to see the absurdity of this whole situation: I'm just hiding, in a ridiculous helmet, with a camouflage vest, leaning on a pallet.

I hear footsteps in the distance. The noise of the game. Trotting, yelling, laughter, high fives. I come back to reality. I try to stand up. My legs are mine once again. I grip the pallet to give me a boost. It's fine. I can do this. I'll get out on the front line, let someone shoot me, and then watch the rest of the game from the sidelines. I want some chocolate. I'm thirsty and want to puke at the same time. I stand up from my hiding spot; I see a person trying to hide behind some bushes. I don't think: I aim and shoot. From behind the hiding place, a familiar head appears, then the body. It's Maika.

"Marisa?" she says incredulously. "What the fuck are you doing? Are you an idiot?"

"Shit, Maika, sorry, I didn't see you clearly," I answer, trying not to sound stoned.

"But I've been calling you for forever! I can't believe this." Maika is incredibly pissed off. Smoke is coming out of her ears.

Maika is one of those people who doesn't know how to lose: not at work and not in life, and especially not in this strange cocktail of work and life. She looks at me, expressionless, lifts her rifle, points directly at my head, and shoots. I duck.

"What the hell are you doing?!" I scream. "Not at the head or the eyes!"

Maika shoots again. I hide as best I can. I'm starting to retch and I break into a cold sweat. Maika appears out of nowhere and points at me with her rifle again, right between the eyes, staring at me with the most scathing look I've ever seen. Suddenly she frowns, something flutters through her mind, and her face completely transforms. Maybe it was sanity. Now she is looking at me with pity, as if she just found a fawn in the middle of the forest. Finally, she lowers her rifle.

"Are you OK, Marisa?" She kneels down and puts her hand on my knee. "You don't look well, you're yellow."

"I'm dizzy and nauseous," I respond, touching my forehead and taking off the helmet. "Sorry, I didn't see you clearly."

"OK, OK, don't worry, I'm going to call for help." Maika stands up and waves her arms in the air. She yells "Truce!" and disappears.

Three minutes later, Maika reappears with the monitor who'd given us the pep talk at the start of the game. He's about twenty-three, with a mullet and earrings made out of coconuts. I suppose that, for the rest of my life, I'll have to pretend that Maika isn't a complete psychopath.

"Hello, I'm Emilio."

"Hello, Emilio."

"Are you OK?"

"I'm feeling dizzy."

"Did you have breakfast this morning?"

"Honestly, no."

And then Emilio moves closer and starts sniffing me like a wild animal. He knows, and I know he knows.

"You can leave us alone," he tells Maika. "I'll take care of this."

"She shot me by mistake, because she was like she is now, a bit out of it." Maika glances at her red paint stain. "Can I keep playing?"

Emilio looks at Maika and seems to understand the kind of

person she is. He pulls a yellow sticker out of his backpack and puts it on top of the stain, indicating that she can rejoin the game. Maika smiles.

"Thanks! Feel better, Marisa." And she leaves.

"Hey, sorry for asking, but did you smoke some weed?"

"Yes."

"OK." Emilio looks into my eyes and then glances around to make sure no one is overhearing. "You know you're just greening out, right?"

"Yes."

"OK, I'm going to take you to the hotel and order you an orange juice and a pastry. You'll be fine after you eat."

He helps me up, puts my arm around his neck, and we slowly walk back. War wound. I've fought bravely. For some reason, there with Emilio, I'm starting to feel better.

"Let's take this other path so we don't run into anyone."

"Thanks."

The day is sunny and cloudless. In the background, I can hear my coworkers shouting. But the noises fade as we go down the other path. I can't hear a thing. Not even the birds. I wonder if anyone's ever done a study on the relationship between adventure sports and the flight of local fauna to less populated, calmer spaces. Imagine being a starling and having a group of executives show up every weekend and start shooting at each other. It must be the animal kingdom equivalent of your upstairs neighbor vacuuming on Saturday mornings.

We enter the hotel lobby, and Emilio sits me down on one of the peach-colored sofas. He heads to the reception desk and then comes to sit beside me. A minute later, a very friendly young woman appears with a juice and a chocolate chip muffin. I take a few sips of juice and start to pull the muffin apart.

"Hey, sorry for asking," says Emilio, "but . . ."

I look at Emilio as I drink. Now I'm the one who knows.

"You want a joint?"

He smiles nonchalantly and shrugs. If only I could be in my early twenties again: that ease, that tranquility, that radiant gaze, still crystal clear. The feeling of possibility, of having your whole life and all your options ahead of you. The serenity to ask a stranger for a joint because life can only offer up good things. I put the cup down and start to open my fanny pack.

"No, no . . . not here."

"OK, well, let me finish my muffin and we'll go to my room."

Emilio nods, complicit. It's interesting how easily trust is established between two drug addicts: in a nightclub bathroom or in the lobby of a Segovian hotel, same difference.

"Can you order me another one?" I ask him. "And another juice?"

Emilio gets up obediently and again speaks with the clerk. He smiles at her, winks—he's clearly won her over. Oh, for the self-confidence of a gregarious, tanned, twenty-three-year-old guy. The world smiles on guys like Emilio. They can go wherever they want, do whatever they want, and always land on their feet. He soon returns and holds out his hand. I grasp it. He tells me that room service will bring up a full breakfast soon. We walk through the hallway as if we were lifelong friends, but as soon as we step in my room, Emilio is gobsmacked.

"Whoa, not too shabby, huh?"

"You haven't seen it before?"

"No, we just come in for the special activities, and they're usually outside. I've never come up to a room."

I pull the joint out of my fanny pack and pass it to him. Emilio goes over to the window, opens it, and lights the joint as if he'd been doing exactly that all his life: smoking weed with strange women in hotel rooms.

"Hey, sorry to ask, but what do you do?"

"I'm head of creative strategy," I say like a good girl who's been taught how to respond politely to adults. I'm seven years old, I'm in fifth grade, and I'm head of creative strategy.

"Whoa, that's a big deal, right?"

"No, it just sounds like one." I walk over to the window and inhale the smoke he's exhaling. "What do you do?"

"I'm a monitor for outdoor activities," he says, taking another hit.

"Well, just call yourself a leisure activities instructor or something like that."

Emilio stares at me for a second and then starts cracking up.

"You're right, that's so stupid." His laughter is contagious, so I laugh too.

Someone knocks on the door.

"That must be the breakfast manager," I say.

Emilio laughs with the goofiness of a really high person and waves his hand around frantically as if that could get rid of the smell. I signal for him to keep quiet, but he can't stop laughing. Outside, through the peephole, I see the same friendly blonde from the reception desk, waiting with a little cart.

"Just leave it there, thanks," I tell her. "I'm in my robe."

Emilio watches me from the window as he takes an enormous hit. What would a cute twenty-something guy think of the woman in front of him? Do I seem fun, hip, cool? Do I seem different than my coworkers? Does he see me? Or am I just another ridiculous executive who doesn't know how to smoke a joint without greening out?

"You're a good liar." He takes another hit, exhaling as if he'd smoked all the marijuana in Segovia. Then he goes to the bathroom and flushes the roach. "I'd better get back."

"Cool. I think I'm going to sleep a little."

Emilio nods. His eyes are glassy and he smiles. I walk him to the door and he helps me get the cart inside.

"Nice to meet you."

He smiles at me. I smile at him. Then he draws closer and kisses me. At first I pull away, but then I just go with it. The chaste kiss turns into a full-on make-out, but instead of trying to take it any further, Emilio pulls back and smiles at me again.

"Hasta la vista, baby."

"Bye."

I close the door. Hasta la vista, baby? In my room, alone again, I eat some scrambled eggs and pancakes with chocolate syrup and bacon, and my body starts to return to its old self. When I've finished, I close the curtains, take off my clothes, and slip into the soft sheets. I unplug the hotel phone so no one can call me. On my cell, I put on a YouTube video of birds of prey, and I drift off to sleep with the distant murmur of my coworkers finishing the paintball game.

X

I stare at the crown moldings around the ceiling. It's 6:15 in the evening. Light slips through the curtains. A gentle breeze travels through the room. For a brief moment, I feel peace. I think of the aphorism "Fake it till you make it." The idea is that if you follow the rules of the game, pretend to be confident, competent, and knowledgeable, in the end you'll become the person you're pretending to be. Acting like a winner until you win, until the container becomes content. I have a rule inspired by that: fake it until people leave you alone. You can't change the world; you can only try to keep the world from changing you.

I have a WhatsApp from Ramón asking me how I'm doing. There's another from Pablo asking if I've killed myself yet. I have a text from my phone company saying I can get more data if I send an SMS that says "GOLDEN HOUR." I have a silenced WhatsApp group with people from the office, with sixty-eight new messages. They've sent photos from earlier today, all looking sweaty, smiling, and splotched with red or blue paint. I'm not in any of the photos. What would happen if I just disappeared without a trace? Who would notify the police? Would they give them the photo from my work

ID, or would they take something off my Instagram? What would be the theory about my disappearance? Would they also think it was suicide? Who would let my parents know? How many people would attend my funeral? I quickly google how much coffins cost and find out they're really expensive. I'm sure my mother would mutter "Outrageous!" when she saw those prices. I decide it's better to take a shower and wash away my negative thoughts. At seven, there's a cocktail hour and then the speeches.

When I get out of the shower, I put on a red dress with white daisies, some Mary Janes, a little blush and mascara, and I go down to the lobby. Several coworkers ask me how I'm feeling. I tell them I'm fine, that I'd skipped breakfast and got dizzy. A lie repeated a thousand times becomes truth, as some Nazi said. A series of very smiling and solicitous waitresses offer us wine and beer on trays. There are also some dubious canapés. I grab a teriyaki chicken skewer and a glass of white wine.

"Marisa! How are you? You had us worried." It's Ramón. He's wearing a beige linen suit that makes him look like a sex tourist.

"Fine, fine, I didn't have any breakfast."

"Breakfast is the most important meal of the day, Marisa."

"And swimming is the most complete sport."

Ramón nods with satisfaction.

"Indeed, Marisa, indeed."

The waitresses tell us that it's time to go into the event room. I put several canapés on a napkin, ask them to refill my wine, and go in to look for a seat. I sit in the corner in case I need to flee. The event room is dimly lit. I look around; my coworkers are chatting and smiling, seemingly in their element. I have the feeling that they're more relaxed than I am, maybe because they've bonded over shooting each other all morning.

"Is this seat free?" It's Carlos.

I nod.

"Great, thanks."

I make room for him to pass, but he invites me to scooch over to the empty spot right beside him. And I do. I've fallen into his trap almost without realizing.

"What's up? Are you feeling OK?"

"Yeah, I just didn't have any breakf . . ."

My words are drowned out by the deafening sound of "Viva La Vida," by Coldplay, coming from the loudspeakers. I drink my wine and look around at my coworkers clapping like automatons. A man of about sixty-five, wearing a black suit and sneakers, comes running in from the back and leaps up onto the stage with an agility that shocks me; he starts clapping and invites everyone to stand up and applaud, and to my surprise, people do. He runs from one side of the stage to the other, clapping, leaping, and smiling like a lunatic. Suddenly the music stops.

"Let me tell you a story, and listen up!" he says through a microphone that is too loud. "A few years ago, I was interviewing for a personal assistant. Of course, my human resources team, or, as I like to call them, my guardian angels, made a preselection . . . but I wanted to have final say on the candidate who would be working shoulder to shoulder with me, who would be responsible for my personal schedule and my trips, and would be sending my wife flowers on her birthday."

People laugh, of course, at the joke about useless men who can't remember important dates.

"So I found myself with three résumés on my desk, and of the three people I had to interview that morning, let me confess to you, I already had a favorite."

I'm impressed by how the man's tone of voice and timing are exactly what I'm used to seeing in TED Talks. I would even say that his story is the same: the typical tale of prevailing, with an impactful surprise ending.

"My favorite was a thirty-seven-year-old man, with a lot of

experience as an executive assistant at a well-known law firm, who also volunteered every summer with NGOs in Africa . . . Lesson number one!" shouts the man suddenly, creating an anticipatory silence. "We are what we do and, often, what we do outside of work says more about us than our work itself. What did it tell me about that person? That he was compassionate, that he liked helping, that he would rather spend his summers on humanitarian work than sunbathing and drinking margaritas."

People laugh again, as if sunbathing and drinking margaritas and not being productive outside of work were a mortal sin.

"All right. Of course my guardian angels didn't make it easy for me: the other two candidates were also excellent, and the truth is, I haven't the slightest doubt that any of the three candidates could have perfectly carried out the job. The first one who showed up was a young man, a recent university graduate, dean's list, he'd done an internship, but according to what he told me, he felt he was more than prepared for his first real job. I liked his self-confidence and ease, I liked seeing a young person with such clear ideas . . . Lesson number two!" he again howls at us, who are by now completely absorbed in his monologue. "Dress for the job of your dreams. And I'm not just talking about clothes, but your entire being: you aren't an inexperienced young person, you are a young person in search of your first experience."

The speaker paces and looks down at his feet, pensive, giving us time to calmly assimilate the cockamamie self-help shit he'd just said.

"The second candidate was a woman of about forty. She hadn't gone to university, but she had a lot of experience: the company where she'd worked for twenty years had closed due to the recession, and after taking a few months of rest, she began looking for a new position. I asked them both: 'What are your hobbies?' The young man told me that he liked spending time with his girlfriend and his friends. Normal, of course—he was a young man. The woman told me that, most of all, she liked to spend her free time with her children. Normal, of course—she was a mother. And do you know what? There's nothing bad about either of those answers; quite the contrary, I'm a big supporter of family values . . . but neither of their responses surprised me. Neither of them left me with my mouth hanging open. Neither of them made me stand up, walk out of my office, and tell my guardian angels: 'Draw up a contract right now!' Lesson number three! Impact!" He bangs hard on the microphone. "Impact! Impact! We all have an opportunity, just one, to stand out from the other candidates. Are you a surfer? Tell me about it! You love sushi? Tell me about it! Are you learning Chinese? Tell me about it! Leave me remembering you, wanting to know more, leave me with the feeling you're a dynamic, productive, capable person, with interests . . . and not some slacker who spends evenings watching TV with his girlfriend."

More laughter from my coworkers. I cannot believe it.

"When it came time to interview the third candidate, he didn't show. Well, being five minutes late is understandable, fifteen is disrespectful, an hour is almost an insult, but this candidate didn't show up until the next day, apologizing, of course, and when my guardian angels told me he was downstairs, I saw him in . . . and then he told me a story." Another dramatic pause. "'Sir, first of all, forgive me for not showing up yesterday: on my way to the interview, since I was early, I decided to have a coffee in a café nearby and, just as I was about to leave, a woman fainted and I went over to help her. You see, I did a first aid course so I could work with an NGO in Africa, and since there was no doctor around, I stayed with her until the ambulance arrived, and before I realized it, two hours had passed. So I went back home, crestfallen, and when I told my wife what had happened, she said, "Go and tell the story to your interviewer; if he's a good man, he'll understand." And that's what I'm doing.' In that moment I got out of my chair, shook his hand, and said, 'Congratulations, the job is yours.' The man, who's still my assistant to this day, said, 'Really? How is that possible?' And I told him, 'Because God sees all, and that woman that you helped yesterday was my wife.'"

"Viva La Vida" starts playing again, a song I'm completely sure he doesn't have the rights to use. People start clapping, and suddenly the man is leaping again and shouting messages like "HELPING OTHERS IS HELPING YOURSELF!" "THE WAYS OF THE LORD ARE INSCRUTABLE AND SO ARE THE WAYS OF COMPANIES." I want to dig a hole in the marble floor and hide underground.

I look around, appalled, I can't believe people are buying this load of horseshit, but everyone is looking at him like he's Jesus Christ. I assume Ramón opted for the divinity coach: the priest turned president of a multinational or something. That, of course, is the first thing he shares after the story of the Good Samaritan: how first he met Jesus and then he met his wife, and how God taught him to run his company according to the Ten Commandments. His talk continues along the same paths: all his stories are improbable parables from which he extracts a series of lessons that mix God with the IBEX 35 or the lepers with interns. He talks about Jesus Christ as a model of the perfect leader, a humble person who serves others. He talks about small companies facing multinationals with references to David and Goliath. Between one story and the next, Coldplay sounds out, and he leaps and gambols. Toward the end, he just shouts over Coldplay, phrases like "GOD WILL MAKE YOU FREE," "FOLLOW YOUR DREAMS," "TREAT OTHERS WELL," "BE A GOOD PERSON."

I wonder how much money that twit has pocketed by saying all this stupid shit without blinking. The talk hadn't been more than forty-five minutes, and I feel I've aged nineteen years. I look around: people are ecstatic. I gesture to Carlos to let me out so I can scamper down the hallway and grab a glass of wine to tolerate the next speaker.

"Marisa!" Ramón exclaims when I'm almost at the door. I approach him. "Warm up, you're on next."

"What?" I look at him, confused. "Now? Don't we have another speaker?"

Ramón observes me irritably, takes me by the elbow like a nun in a Catholic school, and leads me outside.

"Didn't you read my last email?"

"What email?"

"The second speaker canceled on us, we're substituting his talk with yours, and then we'll have the concert."

"And I'm up now? After that guy?" I look at him, horrified.

"Yes, you don't mind, do you? You've got everything ready?"

"Sure, sure, I have to go up to the room for my computer and things, but I've got everything ready."

"Don't worry, you have fifteen minutes."

Fuck. Fuck. Fuck. Playing office is easy if you know how, but sometimes the game catches you unprepared; sometimes you feel like a clumsy kid with chubby cheeks who gets picked last in PE because he always drops the ball; sometimes it's like a water balloon that soaks your Sunday-best dress, like the jump rope that gets tangled in your legs and makes you fall to the ground and your last two baby teeth go flying through the air.

I go up to the room at top speed. I sit at the desk and open my laptop. I'm going on stage in fifteen minutes, and all I have is the title: "BEING CREATIVE IS EASY IF YOU KNOW HOW." I start to copy and paste some Google results into a PowerPoint. I add a few GIFs, some bright colors, enormous attention-grabbing headlines, stock photos. I touch my chest and note some slight tachycardia. I glance around for my Ativans, and then I notice my fanny pack. A thought races through my mind like a bullet. What if . . . ?

I cautiously stand up and stroll through the room in a very delicate emotional state. I sit on the edge of the bed with the fanny pack in my hands, unzip it, and review the arsenal. There are a couple of bags of molly. I stick my pinky finger into one and bring some to my tongue. It's better if I get loose and perky than if I fall asleep on stage. The idea is still in my head, but it hasn't yet taken shape. How many pills are in here? Is Pablo a dealer? Think, Marisa, think. Playing office is easy if you have sufficient means. Maybe it's easier to impress all those people if you influence them somehow. If, let's just say, they have an unforgettable, pleasurable, luminous experience for the first time in their lives. Maybe the only thing you need is an illusion: lights, music, and action. I look into the mirror, and suddenly I'm aware that I'm going to do it.

I get into the elevator with my laptop under my arm and the fanny pack around my waist. When the doors open, I see my coworkers in the lobby, enjoying some canapés between one spectacle and the next, going over to chat and, worst of all, to take selfies with the Catholic twit who just gave that talk. I ask Ramón for a few minutes to prepare and tell him I'll let them know when everything is ready.

"Hi," I say to a passing waitress. "I'm the next speaker, can you help me with some things?"

"Sure!" she answers with an angelic smile. "Just tell me what you need."

"I need juice, do you have juice?"

"Sure, of course."

"OK, well, some juice and like thirty little plastic cups, please."

"What kind of juice?"

"I don't know, what's your favorite?"

"Pineapple?"

"All right, pineapple."

I go into the events room and take the stage. I plug in my

laptop so it projects on the main screen and then I walk over to the light switches at the back. There are a set of colored lights, probably meant for couples' dances at cheesy weddings, and I turn them on. Some spotlights in red, blue, and green move over the main stage. I shut them off. On the back screen, I can see the first slide of my presentation: "BEING CREATIVE IS EASY IF YOU KNOW HOW (I PROMISE!)." The waitress diligently comes in with three enormous pitchers of pineapple juice on a tray.

"The cups are over there, would you like me to help you pour?"

"No, no, I can do it myself."

"OK, just let me know if you need anything."

"Thank you."

I close the doors to the events room. The back of my neck is sweating; my hands are trembling. I approach the small table with the three pitchers of pineapple juice, and I pull out the contents of my fanny pack. I crush up a bag with ten or twelve pills in it, and I mix that into the two little bags of MDMA. Next I pour it all into the pitchers and stir the contents with straws that will end up killing some dolphins in the Pacific. I take a deep breath, wipe the sweat dripping down my forehead, and then clean the sweat from my hands on my dress. The die is cast. I call for the waitress.

"I want you to serve juice to the entire audience. It's important."

The waitress nods.

"If you want, I'll hand out the cups and you serve the juice," I suggest. I turn toward the hall, where all my coworkers are. "Come in one by one, please!"

My coworkers diligently form a single line. As they enter, I give them a plastic cup and smile. Next to me, the waitress serves them a splash of juice. For some reason, either the spirit of camaraderie created that morning or the epileptic attack provoked by the divinity coach, no one finds it odd, and some are already starting to drink. The waitress empties the first, second, and third pitcher until everyone is holding a little cup. Will this work? I hope so.

I see a few surprises among the familiar faces: the previous speaker and Emilio, who winked at me as he entered and sat close to the door. I take a deep breath and head up to the stage. On the screen appears the title along with a GIF of a dog typing on a computer. I approach the microphone.

"Good evening, everyone," I say timidly. I swallow hard. I force myself to breathe deeply, the way they teach you in Pilates. Here goes nothing: "Many of you already know me, you know that my name is Marisa, but perhaps some of you aren't very clear on what it is that I do. Which is totally normal—my mother still isn't very clear on it either." Laughter from the back, good. "I'm a creative strategist, which means I elaborate creative ideas and strategies for our clients or, to put it another way, I'm the person you call when you find out a brand has a ton of money and doesn't know how to spend it." More laughter. My tongue is limber; I feel like I'm starting to loosen up. I crack my knuckles: the spectacle begins. "Throughout my life, I've been asked on many occasions"—none, to be exact—"what is the secret to creativity, or what makes a normal person become a creative person, and I always say the same thing." I move on to the next slide: a stock image of a man in a suit looking furiously at his computer. "Have you been hydrating today?" Dramatic pause, I pace the stage while staring at the audience, transforming into a TED Talk speaker in San Francisco. Just like Elena said: life is a performance. "Seems silly, right? But let's take a moment, before we do anything else, to drink the juice you were given, and I'll tell you how the human body works."

People smile, look around somewhat uncomfortably, but soon the first sips begin.

"Come on! It's not like it's a cup of cement! Why is it so hard for us to carry out some of the most basic tasks? Most of us know that the brain is made up of eighty percent water, but numerous studies have shown that we don't drink enough to properly function; you know the old refrain about two liters of water a day. We wouldn't struggle so much if they were two liters of beer, right?" More laughter. Who do I think I am? Jerry Seinfeld? "If we don't drink water, we don't hydrate our brain, and a dehydrated brain is the number one enemy of a creative person, according to science." Next slide: Ally McBeal's dancing baby appears, bouncing and swaying in the corners of the slide. "Next question: Have you done something today that has nothing to do with work? Inspiration doesn't abide by schedules and routines. You can't ask a musician to deliver a song between nine and five next Thursday, right?"

People nod. I continue.

"You wouldn't say to a poet: I need a sonnet about the arrival of spring today before two. You can't demand that creatives work on a schedule either! But we live in a society ruled by the hands on a clock, and clients have their deadlines, so we force our creativity. So, I'll ask again, have you done anything today that has nothing to do with work? I have! I danced!" I hit play, and a horrible song by Sia and David Guetta—which I, of course, don't have the rights to either—starts blaring. "Every morning, after reading my work emails, before I leave for the office, I listen to this song . . . and I dance. Come on! Stand up, everybody!"

I'm surprised when everyone stands up with no complaint. I imagine the previous speaker, the wine, and the mix of ecstasy and pineapple juice have quashed all embarrassment. I crank up the music and turn on the colored lights.

"Let's dance!"

People start dancing like in a small-town festival, sort of

tense at first, but as the song progresses, they start enjoying themselves. Some people even close their eyes and run their hands over their bodies; there are open mouths, people high-fiving with just their fingertips. I get the lights going faster.

"That's it!"

When the song ends, they're all standing, as if waiting for the next one, until gradually they sit back down in their plastic chairs.

"Good job, guys, good job," I say, noticing that I'm starting to slightly slur my words, not as if I were totally wasted on molly, but more like as if I were from Lyon. "Third question: When's the last time you had a good laugh? A hydrated, unstressed, relaxed, and happy brain tends to be more creative." I go over to my laptop and put on a compilation of fat people falling.

I observe the audience laughing their heads off, contracting their sphincters, rolling in their seats, wiping away tears. It's a magnificent spectacle—humans are incredible. When the video ends, I stare at my coworkers again.

"Numerous studies have shown the mental and emotional benefits of laughter. Laughter works more than a thousand muscles in the body; in other words, it gets us physically active. Not only that, but it rids us of stress and anxiety. And the most interesting part is that we can induce it in ourselves, free, for zero euros . . . Don't tell that to our clients!"

The audience is on top of the world. I switch to the next slide: a watermarked photo of a black notebook; you can start to see I was in a rush.

"Next question: Do you take notes? It's true that some of our best ideas come when we're in the bathroom or sleeping. A creative person jots down absolutely every idea that runs through their head. My house is filled with notebooks, and I always sleep with one by my bed." I bring my index finger up to my chin and I observe the audience, as if I were the Steve Jobs portrait on his book cover. "Every idea, as stupid as it might seem, can be the seed of a better idea. And, lastly, have a good team." The next slide shows a group of white people in suits, in an office, holding up their fingers in the victory sign. "You're nobody without a great team behind you. That silly idea you wrote down at midnight can be the spark that ignites someone else's mind. Remember the famous phrase that Steve Jobs said before he invented the iPhone: 'If you walk alone, you'll get there faster; if you walk with others, you'll get farther.'" I take a dramatic pause that gives me enough time to pray that no one searches for whether Steve Jobs actually said that. "Thank you all very much."

People applaud. I leave up a summary slide that reads: "DRINK WATER, DANCE, LAUGH, WRITE, AND BE A GOOD PERSON, PLEASE." I put on a playlist of hits from the aughts, turn the small-town disco lights back on, and leave the stage.

"That was fabulous, Marisa!" exclaims Ramón, his eyes like two lighthouses.

"Thanks so much!"

"That was awesome, Marisa," says Maika, approaching me with a half smile and kissing me on the corner of my mouth. "Ooh, sorry, hahahaha, well, you know what they say, fighting is often a sign of suppressed desire." She winks at me. "Hahahaha."

The staff enters the events room and starts diligently clearing away the chairs, creating a dance floor. They start placing bottles of alcohol and soda and cups and ice on a table in the back. Some of my coworkers go order a cocktail. I remain in the middle of the floor, watching them, like the ugly girl no one ever asks to dance. Or maybe the pretty girl who never dances with anyone. I get a few more congratulations and, to my surprise, I'm feeling some sort of pride. Survivor's pride, maybe. Suddenly, the music stops. Ramón is on the stage with a microphone in his hand. The surprise of the night.

"Colleagues. Or, at this point, I should say *friends.*" Ramón smiles.

People applaud; someone yells out, "Three cheers for the coolest boss: Ramón!"

"I want to thank you for today. I know it wasn't easy for us to make time to be together, but I think our efforts have been rewarded tenfold. I want to thank Federico Infante, our divinity coach, for giving us a talk we'll never forget." Certainly not. "And thanks as well to our colleague Marisa, who's given us a master class in what it takes to become a creative person. A round of applause for them both."

People start clapping and looking over at us. I smile timidly and say thank you. I'm not used to public displays of gratitude, but it feels better than I'd imagined it would. Or maybe it's the drugs.

"And now, to top it all off, I want to introduce our final guest. We added a concert to finish off this fantastic event, a gift for our employees, who work so hard every day. So, please, enjoy the rest of the evening. Tomorrow we'll head out at 12:30, so also enjoy the delicious hotel breakfast and, if you have time, the spa." More applause. "And, without further ado . . . let's welcome the finalist in the thirteenth season of the show *Born to Shine,* known for his hit 'Happy Little Heart' and a solid candidate to represent Spain in a future Eurovision. Give it up for José Carlos Ruiz!"

We applaud the man, who gets on stage euphorically, wearing a white suit and matching hat, and begins playing the first chords of "Happy Little Heart," which is the only song that any of us might know from him. That doesn't matter. We've decided to go all in and it's a wild scene. Groups are dancing together. Maika grabs my arm. "Come on, Marisa, let's shake our booties!"

I start dancing with the sales team. Every time my eyes meet one of my coworkers', they raise their drinks or smile at me and, gradually, I start to respond in kind. Imitating them and trying not to think about how ridiculous this situation is, I swing my hips to the rhythm of "Happy Little Heart," already on its second encore. "A happy little heart, a tender little heart, even over harsh winters, a heart that never splinters." I can't help but laugh as I sing along.

For a moment, I wonder what Rita would think if she were here and saw me like this, laughing as I twerk with Maika and Sonsoles from HR. Maybe she would dance too. That's the thing about drugs: they make you want to dance. "A once barren little heart," croons José Carlos Ruiz at the song's bridge, "also blooms in spring." The lyric isn't quite right, but I get what he means. "An empty little heart can also become full." I look at Maika, whose eyes are filled with tears, and she grabs me by the neck.

"Isn't this just the sweetest song, Marisita?"

I chuckle. We are not of the same species, but maybe we can find a middle ground. I think about all those YouTube videos I've watched about the animal world. I think about mutualism: when different species help each other for a common benefit, like the sea anemone, a poisonous marine animal with large tentacles, and the clownfish, which is immune to its venom. The anemone's poison protects the fish from predators. The fish, in turn, protects the anemone from other fish that feed on it. I look at Maika and the rest of my coworkers. Maybe they're my anemones, protecting me in an aseptic work environment, safe from the dangers of unemployment. Although, seeing them like this (unintentionally drugged out of their gourds, resolutely drunk, dancing ridiculously, free, a bit flustered, shameless), they are more like the clownfish. I think of how often we've read about the big fish eating the little fish, when maybe we're all confused tiny fish in the tank of some multimillionaire, getting along as best we can, helping each other as best we can, trying to survive.

Now the almost winner of a reality show that no one watches has decided to sing hits of yesteryear, today, and forever that he must've played in one of the final rounds. My coworkers dance and sing along, whisper in huddles, laugh their asses off.

I look at the full room and think that if I were to disappear today, maybe they would give a shit. They would say the last thing they remembered about me: "Marisa was fun and very creative."

I slowly separate from the group, telling them that I need to get some fresh air, which is true. Along the way, my coworkers pat me on the back and smile. They make affectionate remarks. In the background, I hear someone make a toast—"To the team!" "To the best team!"—and little by little, I leave all that commotion behind. I emerge into the cool night, silent except for the crickets. I sit on a small bench by the porch and stare up at the stars illuminating the darkness. Echoes of laughter reach me from inside. I think about pretense: about the things we do to feel other things. Wake up, shower, get dressed and ready, fantasizing that maybe today will be different. I wonder if faking could end in real feeling. I wonder if, deep down, everyone isn't just as desperate to feel something else: the void in your stomach the first time you go on a roller coaster, the warmth you feel when you return home after a few weeks away. I remember that feeling. It must be somewhere.

My eyelids start to feel heavy. Today I faked it, and later I lived too. I ran. I smoked a joint. I had a green-out in the middle of the forest. I kissed a stranger. I connected with my coworkers, even though I had to drug them. Without realizing it, I fall into a deep sleep.

When I wake up, the sky is beginning to lighten. I'm alone and barefoot, covered in a shawl. I look around me, but I am completely alone. I take the shawl in my hands and, somewhat confused, bring it up to my nose. I smell Maika's perfume. I go up to my room with the shawl over my shoulders. The hotel is now silent. In the elevator, I look at myself in the mirror and I realize I look really good. Despite everything, it wasn't a bad day.

Part Two

OOTO

FROM: recursos.humanos@publiciyas.com
TO: directores@publiciyas.com
SUBJECT: Internal investigation team-building retreat

Good morning,

After receiving a series of complaints by one of the speakers and someone in our team, we hereby inform all those who attended the team-building retreat last weekend that we are opening up an internal investigation in order to clarify the events.

Your well-being is of the utmost importance and, as such, as a first step we are making available free testing, which will be treated in the highest confidence, conducted by the RoMeCor analysis laboratory. Testing will take place in the employee cafeteria starting at 9:15.

We will send more information through this channel as soon as it becomes available.

Best regards,
Sonsoles

FROM: marisa@publiciyas.com
TO: recursos.humanos@publiciyas.com; directores@
publiciyas.com
SUBJECT: OOTO

Hello!

I'm out of the office and mostly offline until Monday, September 6th. For any urgent matters please write to ramon@publiciyas.com or to natalia.dominguez@ publiciyas.com.

Thank you.

FROM: ramon@publiciyas.com
TO: recursos.humanos@publiciyas.com; directores@
publiciyas.com
SUBJECT: Internal investigation team-building retreat

????????

What does this mean, Sonsoles? Laboratory analysis of what? Are we in danger?

I need more information, I'm completely lost here.

kind retards,

FROM: marisa@publiciyas.com
TO: recursos.humanos@publiciyas.com; directores@
publiciyas.com
SUBJECT: OOTO

Hello!

*I'm out of the office and mostly offline until Monday,
September 6th. For any urgent matters please write
to ramon@publiciyas.com or to natalia.dominguez@
publiciyas.com.*

Thank you.

FROM: maika@publiciyas.com
TO: recursos.humanos@publiciyas.com; directores@
publiciyas.com
SUBJECT: Internal investigation team-building retreat

Ramón I'll come by your office and explain. xx

Sent from my iPhone

FROM: marisa@publiciyas.com
TO: recursos.humanos@publiciyas.com; directores@
publiciyas.com
SUBJECT: OOTO

Hello!

*I'm out of the office and mostly offline until Monday,
September 6th. For any urgent matters please write
to ramon@publiciyas.com or to natalia.dominguez@
publiciyas.com.*

Thank you.

FROM: recursos.humanos@publiciyas.com
TO: directores@publiciyas.com
SUBJECT: Internal investigation team-building retreat

Hello again,

*Given the seriousness of this matter, we want to underscore
the importance of all information remaining on one
channel to avoid duplications. We are in touch with
our legal team, and soon they will give more detailed
information.*

Regards,
Sonsoles

FROM: marisa@publiciyas.com
TO: recursos.humanos@publiciyas.com; directores@
publiciyas.com
SUBJECT: OOTO

Hello!

*I'm out of the office and mostly offline until Monday,
September 6th. For any urgent matters please write
to ramon@publiciyas.com or to natalia.dominguez@
publiciyas.com.*

Thank you.

FROM: eduardo@publiciyas.com
TO: recursos.humanos@publiciyas.com; directores@
publiciyas.com
SUBJECT: Internal investigation team-building retreat

Hello, team:

*On behalf of the financial department we demand a
meeting ASAP to inform us about these events in further
detail. We are completely in the dark here and, obviously,
refuse to submit to any analysis without knowing why. We
demand more transparency.*

FROM: marisa@publiciyas.com
TO: recursos.humanos@publiciyas.com; directores@
publiciyas.com
SUBJECT: OOTO

Hello!

*I'm out of the office and mostly offline until Monday,
September 6th. For any urgent matters please write
to ramon@publiciyas.com or to natalia.dominguez@
publiciyas.com.*

Thank you.

FROM: maika@publiciyas.com
TO: recursos.humanos@publiciyas.com; directores@
publiciyas.com
SUBJECT: Internal investigation team-building retreat

Well said Edu!!! agree 100

Sent from my iPhone

FROM: marisa@publiciyas.com
TO: recursos.humanos@publiciyas.com; directores@
publiciyas.com
SUBJECT: OOTO

Hello!

*I'm out of the office and mostly offline until Monday,
September 6th. For any urgent matters please write*

to ramon@publiciyas.com or to natalia.dominguez@
publiciyas.com.

Thank you.

FROM: legal@publiciyas.com
TO: recursos.humanos@publiciyas.com; directores@
publiciyas.com
SUBJECT: Internal investigation team-building retreat

Good morning,

For the moment, we can say that we are in the process of an
internal investigation. Last Sunday, one of the retreat guests
went to the hospital with generalized complaints and, after
some routine tests, they found a series of illegal substances in
said guest, of which said guest was unaware.

We are requesting the utmost cooperation on the part of
our employees in this process with the relevant authorities
as well as internally, to shine some light on this matter
and take the necessary measures either against the hotel or
against the implicated parties.

We have set up testing with the laboratory Sonsoles
aforementioned, and we ask to be informed if your results
are positive so that we can forward this information to the
National Police Force.

Thank you.

FROM: marisa@publiciyas.com
TO: recursos.humanos@publiciyas.com; directores@
publiciyas.com
SUBJECT: OOTO

Hello!

*I'm out of the office and mostly offline until Monday,
September 6th. For any urgent matters please write
to ramon@publiciyas.com or to natalia.dominguez@
publiciyas.com.*

Thank you.

FROM: ramon@publiciyas.com
TO: recursos.humanos@publiciyas.com; directores@
publiciyas.com
SUBJECT: Internal investigation team-building retreat

dRUGS??????

BEST REGARDS

FROM: marisa@publiciyas.com
TO: recursos.humanos@publiciyas.com; directores@
publiciyas.com
SUBJECT: OOTO

Hello!

*I'm out of the office and mostly offline until Monday,
September 6th. For any urgent matters please write*

to ramon@publiciyas.com or to natalia.dominguez@
publiciyas.com.

Thank you.

FROM: maika@publiciyas.com
TO: recursos.humanos@publiciyas.com; directores@
publiciyas.com
SUBJECT: Internal investigation team-building retreat

I got a call from the speaker's wife!! The priest. The man
almost croaked poor guy and to be honest now that I think
about it i was feeling more ripped than normal, anybody
else???

If our results are positive what do we do?????? go to the ER?

WE DEMAND MORE INFORMATION ABOUT
WHAT IS GOING ON I'VE BEEN AT THIS
COMPANY FOR MORE THAN TWELVE YEARS,
SONSOLES

Sent from my iPhone

FROM: marisa@publiciyas.com
TO: recursos.humanos@publiciyas.com; directores@
publiciyas.com
SUBJECT: OOTO

Hello!

*I'm out of the office and mostly offline until Monday,
September 6th. For any urgent matters please write
to ramon@publiciyas.com or to natalia.dominguez@
publiciyas.com.*

Thank you.

FROM: maika@publiciyas.com
TO: recursos.humanos@publiciyas.com; directores@
publiciyas.com
SUBJECT: Internal investigation team-building retreat

*can we take marisa out of this thread??? I keep getting her
ooto*

Sent from my iPhone

FROM: marisa@publiciyas.com
TO: recursos.humanos@publiciyas.com; directores@
publiciyas.com
SUBJECT: OOTO

Hello!

*I'm out of the office and mostly offline until Monday,
September 6th. For any urgent matters please write
to ramon@publiciyas.com or to natalia.dominguez@
publiciyas.com.*

Thank you.

FROM: legal@publiciyas.com
TO: recursos.humanos@publiciyas.com; directores@
publiciyas.com
SUBJECT: Internal investigation team-building retreat

*From the Human Resources and Legal departments we are
calling an urgent meeting today at 10:30 in the Cibeles
conference room where we will resolve all relevant questions.
Likewise, we will have a member of the National Police
Force in attendance to counsel us on next steps.*

FROM: marisa@publiciyas.com
TO: recursos.humanos@publiciyas.com; directores@
publiciyas.com
SUBJECT: OOTO

Hello!

*I'm out of the office and mostly offline until Monday,
September 6th. For any urgent matters please write
to ramon@publiciyas.com or to natalia.dominguez@
publiciyas.com.*

Thank you.

FROM: claudia@publiciyas.com
TO: recursos.humanos@publiciyas.com; directores@
publiciyas.com
SUBJECT: Internal investigation team-building retreat

*maika let's both look our best for that MEMBER of the
police force ;););)*

FROM: marisa@publiciyas.com
TO: recursos.humanos@publiciyas.com; directores@
publiciyas.com
SUBJECT: OOTO

Hello!

*I'm out of the office and mostly offline until Monday,
September 6th. For any urgent matters please write*

*to ramon@publiciyas.com or to natalia.dominguez@
publiciyas.com.*

Thank you.

FROM: claudia@publiciyas.com
TO: recursos.humanos@publiciyas.com; directores@
publiciyas.com
SUBJECT: Internal investigation team-building retreat

*sorry please disregard the previous email not intended for
the group*

FROM: marisa@publiciyas.com
TO: recursos.humanos@publiciyas.com; directores@
publiciyas.com
SUBJECT: OOTO

Hello!

*I'm out of the office and mostly offline until Monday,
September 6th. For any urgent matters please write
to ramon@publiciyas.com or to natalia.dominguez@
publiciyas.com.*

Thank you.

FROM: maika@publiciyas.com
TO: recursos.humanos@publiciyas.com; directores@
publiciyas.com
SUBJECT: Internal investigation team-building retreat

remove marisa i keep getting autoreplies see you at 10:30!!!

Sent from my iPhone

Part Three

IN ITINERE

It happened the way important things in life usually happen: suddenly. It's human beings, with our need for explanations and closure, who add in those details later, imbuing even the most trivial and banal story with narrative. We look back, rummage around in the drawers of our memory, and determine that it was a certain detail—"He pulled his hand away at the party when his coworker showed up"—that triggered that other thing—"and, in the end, we got divorced." Because in our discombobulated little heads, everything has to have a beginning and an end. A cause and an effect. The world would be a horrible place if we poor mortals didn't have the ability to find some negligible sense in all these haphazard events that are completely irrelevant to the universe.

The story I've been telling myself after what happened is more or less this one:

A woman was walking decisively along a narrow Madrid street that opens onto the Gran Vía. One of those uncomfortable streets filled with dumpsters, scattered trash, cars, scooters, bollards, and scaffolding. One of those streets that have the particular scent of a big city: the aroma of freshly baked bread mixed with the stench of exhaust, rotten banana in the garbage, and cigar smoke, all mixed with the fragrance of the expensive perfume of whoever's just walked past. It was a street that was the polar opposite of the infinite and infinitely lovely beach on Fuerteventura she had just returned from, much to her chagrin. The woman set her feet on the ground as if the ground annoyed her and, in fact, it did annoy her, because she was wearing very uncomfortable sandals with fake leather straps, which chafed both her feet because they'd begun to sweat, and soles as thin as rolling paper, allowing her to feel every little nuisance of city life: the slight heat of a poorly stubbed-out cigarette, the tiny gray rock on her path, the gum that got stuck on her shoe as soon as she'd left the house that she still hasn't managed to get off. And her feet were sweating because it was too hot of a morning for September. A morning that seemed taken from a typical August, one that the calendar couldn't have predicted. And as she walked, irritated with the ground and with her own feet, knowing that it was already too late to go back home and change her shoes, thinking that it was all an attack aimed directly at her, she was so caught up in her own irritation that when she slipped and her purse fell to the ground, at the corner of Gran Vía and San Bernardo, she cursed the air like a lunatic. And the truth is that she was so telescoped by that accrual of aggravations, on the ground gathering up all the items that defined her (the red Yves Saint Laurent lipstick, the datebook, the latest smartphone with an enormous screen that almost made her feel like she was inside the YouTube videos she watched, the tissues, the vape), that she didn't realize nobody could see or hear her until they were in spitting distance. And it was precisely at spitting distance when the only person who should've seen her from farther away finally saw her: the delivery guy who slammed his bicycle into her. The spectacle was quite a sight, as evidenced by the fact that the Gran Vía, noisy as it is, fell silent for a few seconds, like a sign of respect. And the result was a holy mess. The deliveryman, thrown eight meters. The bicycle, encrusted into a store display window. Four pizzas on the crosswalk. A pedestrian saying, "Coulda killed me." The woman in a crumpled heap in the middle of this whole snafu. Cars slamming on the brakes, crashing into each other. One of those cars, swerving just so, but running over something with its back wheels that the driver would remember for the rest of his days: "Something squishy, something human," he would tell his wife that very night. And there was blood, and since blood frightens people, at first no one dared to do anything more than stand and stare. After the initial shock had passed, people soon came to her aid. "Don't move her," advised someone who'd watched a lot of hospital shows on TV. There were several calls for an ambulance. When a man approached the woman in a crumpled heap and asked her how she was feeling, the woman only asked for one thing: "Please, get these fucking sandals off of me." An ambulance soon arrived. The paramedics came rushing out and observed the scene. One went over to the woman; the other went over to the deliveryman. The deliveryman was fine. In shock, but fine. He asked one of those stupid questions that people only ask in very serious moments, which was if he could pick up the strewn pizzas so he could deliver them on time. The woman was worse off, but she found the deliveryman's question so funny when they told her about it on the way to the hospital that anyone paying close enough attention could hear her laughter over the sirens. But that was later. First, and with the utmost urgency, they lifted her onto a stretcher and placed her in the ambulance, which turned on its sirens and disappeared. After a few minutes, the Gran Vía went back to being as it was, the incident entirely forgotten. The witnesses started disappearing from the scene, taking with them a good anecdote to tell over lunch, and the people who hadn't witnessed it began filling the streets without suspecting that a woman had nearly been killed by a man delivering pizzas, for some reason, at nine in the morning. Life, death, and everything in between are not matters we can afford to spend much time lingering on. Everyone has something they need to do. The stores are about to open. People have to get on the metro. The cabbies are starting to get impatient. Hello Kitty and Pikachu are walking toward the Puerta del Sol. The traffic lights turn red and then green. The people saunter; the traffic flows. As if nothing had ever happened.

Or at least that's how I imagined it when I opened my eyes in the hospital after the emergency surgery.

The upshot: dislocated right shoulder, two broken ribs, bruises all over my body, broken right wrist, a cracked hip, and lost index, middle, and ring fingers on my right hand.

Pablo visits and I smile. Elena visits and I smile. My parents visit and they hug me and I smile, nestling into my mother's bosom like a little girl. They spend three nights by my side at the hospital. To my surprise, the immaculately clean hospital is a space where my mother feels safe. On the fourth day, my father starts pacing nervously around the room and complaining of back pain. I tell them it's fine if they return home. They accept in exchange for my promise that I'll spend some time with them, there in my hometown, during my leave. I agree, saying that I'll have all the time in the world. On the day they leave, my mother observes me from the doorway and tells me I didn't cry once, and that I was always a bit odd. I know that's her way of telling me she's happy that I'm not like my cousin Susana.

Then it was time for my coworkers to visit. Natalia comes, as does the rest of my team, now back from their vacations. They all cry and I smile. "It's OK," I tell them. "I'm fine." And I mean it. My coworkers send me a lovely bouquet of flowers that lights up the room, with a note that reads, "Get well soon," but I'm not in any rush to get well. In fact, when I look at my hand, I feel profound bliss at the thought that, maybe, I'll never get well. Ramón visits and plants a kiss on my forehead. "Ay, Marisita, what a disaster." I smile. "Don't worry about a thing, I'll take care of all the paperwork." I smile again. "Ramón," I say, "I don't know if I'm going to be able to return to work." And I hold up my bandaged hand with its enormous gap between the thumb and pinky. "We'll see, Marisita, don't worry about that now, we'll take care of everything," and he plants another kiss on my forehead.

Pablo and Elena come to see me and make plans. Elena says that she can move in with me for a while, Pablo suggests buying a bell so I can ring it when I need him. I say why would I need a bell when I have his phone number, but he says he's already bought it because he thought I would appreciate the eccentricity.

The pain lessens as the days pass, the flowers start to wilt, the visitors become more infrequent, but Elena and Pablo always come. The doctor stares into my eyes and tells me that I'll be on leave from work for a long, long time; then he holds my mutilated hand and says, "A really, really long time, start getting used to the idea." I ask a question I'd been practicing for a moment like this: "Doctor, will I ever play the guitar again?" The doctor shakes his head. Pablo and Elena bite the insides of their cheeks.

One morning, Elena shows up with a picnic basket and a couple of large goose-down pillows she'd just bought at El Corte Inglés. She says one of the reasons I'm not getting better faster is the shitty hospital food and the uncomfortable beds. She pulls the pillows out of their plastic wrapping and fluffs them up with a few punches before positioning them at my back. Then she pulls out some Iberian tomatoes the size of her breasts, cuts them into slices, and dresses them with olive oil and salt. She tells me that she called a lawyer friend of hers, and he said that I could get a ton of money from the delivery company and the driver who ran me over. She mentions an outrageous figure. "With that, and the medical leave for your *in itinere* accident, we could even argue for a permanent leave. You're set for life." I can't believe how luck came into my life, on wheels and with a gig contract.

"Try these tomatoes," says Elena as she patiently places a fork into my left hand. "They're fantastic. I get them at the Mercado de la Cebada; it's one of the few places left in Madrid where the tomatoes still have flavor and actually taste like something, even though they cost half a month's rent."

I sit up. I struggle a bit with the fork because I'm right-handed. Or at least I used to be. Elena tells me I can definitely learn to be a lefty, like lefties used to be forced to learn to be righties so they wouldn't be considered satanic. Pablo shows up with a cold six-pack, offers a beer to Elena, and she says thanks without even looking at him. He cracks open another and places it on my hospital tray with a straw inside. He guzzles down a third. I look at them and realize that we're a family, a strange family.

I think about how in the office they'll always remember me as the person who got run over by a delivery guy and lost three fingers. And that my story will be told forever, to every new hire, every intern. It will be recalled every evening, when the work demands extra hours and someone orders a few pizzas. It will be remembered at every Christmas party, every breakfast celebration, every team-building retreat. And it will be like I'm there, but without me having to be there. I bring a slice of tomato to my mouth.

"Well?" asks Elena, observing me with much ceremony.

I smile. "They're delicious."

Elena pulls out two more forks and offers one to Pablo. She

cuts up a few slices of baguette and some fancy tinned fish and prepares a bowl of fruit to leave in my room. I take another bite of tomato. I've figured it out. In the end, all we need in life is someone who loves us, a bed with nice big pillows, a few cans of cold beer, and tomatoes that still taste like something.

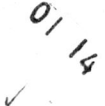

Acknowledgments

First of all, I want to thank my parents. Thank you for awakening my interest from a young age, for supporting me and guiding me, and for buying me every book I wanted on our Saturday morning bookstore visits. I wouldn't be who I am without them.

Secondly, thanks to all the teachers at my school, Nuestra Señora del Socorro, in Benetússer (Valencia), who at some point saw something in me. Particularly my Spanish language and literature teachers, Alfons Garrido and Carmen Alba. And a special mention for my history teacher, who taught me how to see when I only knew how to look: Álvaro Zornoza.

Thirdly, thanks to the good people and even better professionals at this publishing house that has become my home. Thanks to Sergi, for calling me and having faith in that first manuscript I sent him, and to Sandra, for treating it with such care and making it shine.

Fourthly, I want to thank the three friends who read this story even before it was finished. Thanks to Dani, without whose comments and screenshots with "HAHAHA" I wouldn't have had the courage to keep writing. Thanks to Julio, for giving me

---

the confidence I needed, for making toasts with me, and for telling me, "You are a writer." You are my brothers. And thanks to Manu; his raucous laughter in the room next door and his feedback—"fucking awesome" or "not quite"—are what got me to the end. Thank you for what we were.

And, fifthly, thank you, dear reader, for going to a bookstore and giving this little novel a chance amid so many other books on the tables. I hope it has kept you company on the subway or bus, in your doctor's waiting room, on the sofa or in bed before going to sleep. And I hope it was pleasant company. I trust we will meet again.